A dangerous affection . . .

"You have real backbone, Miss Caroline," he said softly, finally managing to take control of his thoughts.

She swallowed, trying to quell the strange sensation in the pit of her stomach. It was the first time he had spoken her name. For some reason, it made her feel rather giddy.

"It's quite easy to appear brave when someone is always coming to the rescue. Once again you had to—how did you put it?—scrape me out of the mud. It must be getting very tiresome."

He mumbled something under his breath.

"I'm sorry to have put you to so much trouble," she continued. "Dear me, it seems to keep getting worse."

Davenport chuckled at that. "Worse? Let me see, I've been engaged in a mad chase on horseback, I've been shot at, punched, and now winged. I figure at this rate I shall be sticking my spoon in the wall by tomorrow."

"No, I—" Her voice caught in her throat.

"I was merely teasing. Don't let me overset you." Was it his imagination, or had her hand brushed up against his cheek in something akin to a caress?

The Hired Hero

Andrea Pickens

A SIGNET BOOK

SIGNET
Published by New American Library, a division of
Penguin Putnam Inc., 375 Hudson Street,
New York, New York 10014, U.S.A.
Penguin Books Ltd, 27 Wrights Lane,
London W8 5TZ, England
Penguin Books Australia Ltd,
Ringwood, Victoria, Australia
Penguin Books Canada Ltd, 10 Alcorn Avenue,
Toronto, Ontario, Canada M4V 3B2
Penguin Books (N.Z.) Ltd, 182–190 Wairau Road,
Auckland 10, New Zealand

Penguin Books Ltd, Registered Offices:
Harmondsworth, Middlesex, England

First published by Signet, an imprint of New American Library, a division of
Penguin Putnam Inc.

First Printing, June, 1999
10 9 8 7 6 5 4 3 2 1

Chapter One

"Is everything all right, Lady Caroline?"

The young lady in question had fairly torn open the letter right in the entrance hall of the imposing manor house in her haste to know its contents. Errant ringlets of honey-colored curls, still damp from the exertion of a hard morning gallop over the fields, obscured part of her face but couldn't hide the furrow that slowly creased her brow as she skimmed the pages.

A look of grave concern came over the butler's craggy face as the furrow deepened. He cleared his throat and spoke again. "I trust that His Grace and the young Viscount are . . . well?" He forbore to say the word "alive" but the slight hesitation in the question made the meaning clear enough.

She raised her eyes from the travel-worn paper. Their rich emerald color, usually vibrant with laughter and high spirits, was clouded, and it seemed to take her a moment to realize she had been spoken to.

"Yes—yes, Papa and Lucien are fine, thank the Lord. It's just that . . ." Her voice trailed off. She abruptly folded the letter and tucked it into the bodice of her navy merino riding habit. "Darwin, will you please find Mrs. Graves," she continued. "Then meet me in the library as soon as possible."

She hurried down the finely appointed hallway and pushed open a massive oak door. The room smelled of beeswax, moroccan leather and the faint, masculine scent of bay rum. Her throat caught at the familiar reminder of her father—this was his favorite spot. She made her way to his ornately carved desk and sat down in front of a banked fire. Despite the warmth emanating from the logs, she couldn't shake the chill she felt creeping over her. Taking out the letter, she smoothed the creased sheets of paper and read them once again. Oh, the words were clear enough. More than clear. Her father was very emphatic about what he wanted her to do.

But why?

She shook her head in consternation. It made no sense. He wanted her to leave Roxbury Manor immediately upon reading his words. She was to travel in an unmarked carriage, without her lady's maid and regular luggage, dressed as plainly as possible, with only the coachman and one of the scullery maids to act as a companion. They were to make all haste to London, stopping only to change horses and for the coachman to grab enough sleep to be able to drive without mishap, yet he wanted them to avoid the main roads. Once in Town, she was to go directly to her uncle Henry and stay there without revealing her presence to anyone until he and her cousin returned from the Continent.

Caroline raised her eyes from the paper and thought for a moment. She was well aware of what her father was involved in. There were too many visits to Whitehall, too many shadowy visitors at odd hours for her not to be aware of his part in the government's efforts to defeat the Little Corsican, now that the rogue had slipped away from Elba and was on the march again. Though he usually credited her intelligence enough to discuss things with her as freely as he did with her cousin Lucien, on this particular mission he had been unusually reticent. Even his sudden departure three weeks ago was prefaced by only a terse explanation that he was needed urgently in Belgium for a short time. It was only slightly mollifying that he told her cousin no more—but Lucien got to go with him. Her eyes narrowed at the thought.

Men. They get to use their wits and have all the adventure.

She sighed and looked back at the last paragraph of the letter. It was even stranger than the preceding ones. Her father wrote that a courier might appear at Roxbury Manor with some papers. While that in itself was not an uncommon occurrence, it was the next lines that sent the chill within her even deeper. The Duke's orders were that, no matter what, the man get himself away from the manor and leave at once for London. He was not to stop until he had delivered what he had to the minister himself—and only him—at Whitehall. Most importantly, he was to be warned to stay on his guard, especially on the road. Then she read the last line.

I beg you do exactly as I ask. Be careful and trust no one.

"Hmmph." Darwin looked over his wire-rimmed spectacles at Lady Caroline Alexandra Georgina Talcott. How well he recognized the set of her jaw and what it meant. He tried to recall when he had first noticed the gesture—it must have been when the lady in question was no more than four years old and had decided that she, too, was ready to ride a horse, just like her older cousin. He nearly smiled, despite the seriousness of the situation. When that look appeared, there was no earthly power he was acquainted with that could stand up to her. He only hoped she had come to the right decision.

"Hmmph," he repeated as he passed the letter to Mrs. Graves, who had served the Duke of Cheviot's family nearly as long as he had. "Your father's orders are quite clear, Lady Caroline." There was a slight pause as he fixed her with a stern look, doing a quite credible job of mimicking the Duke's expression when he was not to be trifled with.

Caroline's face took on an injured look. "I don't willfully disobey my father . . ."

Mrs. Graves snorted. "Like hell ye don't, missy."

"Mrs. Graves! Language, if you please!"

The housekeeper fixed Darwin with a basilisk stare. "Oh, don't be ringing a peal over my head. 'Tis nothing that hasn't tumbled out of her mouth or that of Mr. Lucien more times than can be counted."

Caroline had to suppress a grin. The two old retainers had been going at it for more than her twenty years, or so she had been assured, and the battle showed no signs of abating—she imagined they would be utterly lost without each other.

Mrs. Graves turned her considerable bulk towards Caroline. "And don't ye be putting on that air of innocence. You can hardly think to gammon us! We all know you are wont to do exactly as you see fit, but on this, I agree with Mr. Darwin. You do *exactly* as His Grace says." She shook the letter at Caroline. "I can feel in my bones that something is dreadfully amiss."

Caroline's lips compressed in a tight line. She had sensed that too. There was a strange tone to her father's words, something she had never felt before, as if he were . . . She searched for the right word. Afraid? Certainly not for himself, but for what? Helpless? Because he and Lucien were so far away?

Damnation, she thought, mentally acknowledging that Mrs. Graves was right—her vocabulary did include a number of decidedly unladylike words. Why couldn't her father have told her exactly what was going on? She couldn't help but feel that if it had been Lucien, instead of herself, he would have explained matters more clearly. Her jaw jutted out a fraction farther. Regardless, she would give him no cause to worry. For once, she would do exactly as she was told.

Darwin and Mrs. Graves were watching her intently. Her mouth quirked into a thin smile. "You two needn't look at me as if you were trying to decide just how much rope you'd need to truss me into a carriage."

Darwin let out his breath. "I knew, of course, that your innate good sense would prevail."

"'Course it would," muttered Mrs. Graves. "Females always show more common sense than men when trouble arises."

Darwin shot a quelling look at her, then continued, his tone even more imperious. "Now, it is clear your father wants you to travel incon . . . incock . . ."

"Incognito."

"Precisely, Lady Caroline. Now, there is a small carriage with no crest in storage in the east stable. It will be just the thing." He rang for a footman and gave a number of terse orders. Turning back to Caroline and Mrs. Graves, he added, "John Coachman is a fine driver. He will get you to London and into your uncle's care as quickly as can be done." That he was also a bear of a man and handy with his fives or a pistol was an added benefit, Darwin thought to himself grimly. And like all the rest of the household, he doted on the Duke's only daughter and would do anything to keep her safe.

"Your maid must take your plainest gowns—the grey and olive ones you wear when working in the gardens will do—and alter a seam or two to make them even more unfashionable." Mrs. Graves was not to be denied her part in the planning. "They should be worn enough, though I daresay we could add some fraying at the hem and cuffs."

"I don't know why Papa does not want Mathilde to accompany me . . ."

Mrs. Graves rolled her eyes. "After all these years, Mathilde still can't manage a sentence that makes any sense."

"Mathilde speaks very good English," said Caroline, more out of loyalty than truthfulness. "At least, I understand every word," she added.

"You and only you," observed Darwin. "Besides, you speak French nearly better than she does. The point is, she will attract attention . . ."

"And attention is exactly what His Grace doesn't want," finished Mrs. Graves, ignoring the butler's miffed expression. "You'll take Polly from the kitchen. She's a sensible girl and one who will keep her tongue to herself."

Caroline frowned but didn't argue.

Darwin rose. "I suggest you have Mathilde start on what needs to be done. Have her pack only a small valise, as befitting a country squire's daughter. In any case, you will be in London in a matter of a few days and may send for your things at Grosvenor Square. I want you to leave at first light."

She nodded but couldn't refrain from adding, "I wish Papa had seen fit to explain things to me. If I had a notion of what was going on, perhaps I could think of a way to help him . . ."

"Lady Caroline!" There was a note of warning in Darwin's voice.

"You needn't bellow at me. I said I would do as Papa asks. But this all doesn't make any sense to me. Why should *I* be in any danger?" She looked at the others, the question in her expression as well as her words.

"More than likely His Grace is mistaken, but 'tis better to be cautious. In all likelihood you have nothing to worry about, save for a rather uncomfortable journey back to Town," replied Mrs. Graves, with a bravado that sounded rather hollow to all their ears. Darwin remained silent.

In all his years, he had known the Duke to make precious few mistakes.

Caroline let the book drop in her lap as she stared into the blazing fire. She had come back to the library after supper, knowing full well that sleep would be impossible just yet, even though she must depart at dawn. There were so many questions racing through her mind, not the least of which was why her father was so concerned about this particular messenger. It was not unusual for documents to travel between the Continent, the ministry and the Duke, many of them no doubt sensitive—Caroline had known for some time what sort of work her father was engaged in. No doubt a penchant for ferreting out information ran in the family! So why was this so different . . . ?

A loud noise jarred her from her thoughts. She shot up and hurried into the hallway. The sound was coming from the drawing room. Caroline threw open the door to find that Darwin, armed with a pistol and accompanied by two of the larger footmen brandishing heavy cudgels, was already cautiously approaching the set of French doors that led out to the garden terrace. The banging came again, this time a much weaker sound. Darwin undid the locks and flung the doors open as he stepped back, pistol at the ready.

A body crumpled, face forward, onto the floor. With a muted exclamation of surprise, Darwin knelt beside the motionless form and carefully turned the man over. Caroline, already at the butler's side, was horrified to see an ugly splotch of dark crimson spread across the front of the tattered shirt. The man's face was caked with mud and sweat, his lips chapped and bleeding. "The Duke . . ." he whispered, barely loud enough for them to make out the words. "Papers . . ." His hand clutched weakly at a small oilskin packet hanging by a cord around his neck. A cough wracked the man's frame, bringing a trickle of blood to the corners of his mouth.

"Steady now. You are safe here." Darwin took the man's hand in his own.

The man's eyes fluttered open. "From France. Names . . . he's trying to get . . ." His chest gave a convulsive heave and the faint words trailed off.

"We must send for Dr. Belding immediately," cried Caroline. "The poor man must . . ."

Darwin looked up at her. "I'm afraid it is too late for that." Gently removing the packet from around the man's neck, he straightened and took Caroline by the arm. "Ned and William will see to the poor fellow."

He guided her to the library and then placed the travel-stained packet in the middle of the Duke's desk. They stared at it wordlessly for a few moments.

Darwin cleared his throat. "It seems His Grace had every right to be concerned," he said softly.

Caroline only nodded, then reached out slowly . . .

"Lady Caroline!"

Her hand took up the packet, then she reached for her father's letter opener.

"Lady Caroline!" repeated Darwin. "What in heaven's name do you think you are doing?"

Caroline regarded him calmly, her eyes as steely as her father's. "The man gave his life to get these papers to my father. I have to know what they contain so we may decide what to do."

"You . . . you don't mean to read them?" Darwin's voice cracked slightly.

The letter opener had already severed the thread holding the oilskins together. "That is exactly what I intend to do." Several leaves of thin parchment, folded together and sealed with wax, fell out. Caroline picked them up and, with just a hint of hesitation, broke the seal.

Darwin let out a strangled sigh.

It took only a minute or two to read the contents. Her eyes came up slowly to meet those of the butler. "Good Lord," she breathed. "This is a list of contacts and addresses of our intelligence-gathering rings from Paris to Brussels."

They both looked at each other.

"If it were to fall into the wrong hands, why . . . This must reach my father without fail. Tell Crocket to have the carriage ready to leave as soon as possible."

Darwin seemed to read her mind. "You can't mean to . . ."

"Yes. I mean to take them to London myself."

"Miss Caroline, whoever is after these papers had killed once to get them. He will not hesitate to do so again."

"Yes, and can you imagine how many shall die if he *does* get his hands on them?"

Darwin's lips tightened. "But your father made it clear he didn't want you anywhere near those papers—and with good reason!"

"My father would agree that these papers must get to London, no matter what."

"Miss Caroline." The butler's voice was full of emotion. "I cannot let you let you put yourself in such danger."

"I don't see that you have any choice. Do you think I would be so cowardly as to send one of the grooms or foot-men—or anyone else?" She stared pointedly at him, taking in his reedy legs, slowed now by a touch of rheumatism. "Besides, that would be exactly what our enemy would ex-pect—a lone courier on horseback. On the other hand, I imagine he will not be on the lookout for a nondescript car-riage carrying a lone female and her maid, especially if we stay off the highways."

"She's right, ye know." Mrs. Graves stepped into the room from the shadows of the hall. "Much as it grieves me to say it, I think it is the only decision."

"The Duke would never make such a decision," he argued, though the look on his face was one of resignation.

"The Duke is not here. So it is I who must decide," answered Caroline calmly. "I shall sew the packet into the bodice of my gown—Mathilde is very clever with her needle and fabric. It will be impossible for someone to tell who doesn't know where to look. And after all," she added, "our enemy cannot be entirely sure the papers have reached us."

Darwin pressed his lips together, not ready to give up entirely. "I shall send Tom and Reggie with you as well, armed to the teeth . . ."

She shook her head. "No. That would only attract exactly the sort of attention we wish to avoid." She gave a tight smile to both of them. "Besides, I have a feeling that it is not force we will need to come out on top, but wits."

Caroline sought to find a more comfortable position in the lurching carriage. After nearly two days of continuous travel over rutted back roads, every bone in her body seemed to ache. Things had not gone well from the start. Not many hours after leaving Roxbury Manor, one of the wheels of the old vehicle had come off, nearly oversetting them into a ditch, and costing precious hours before a wheelwright could be found to make things right. Though John Coachman had set a rather breakneck pace after that, it seemed progress was painfully slow. The country roads appeared to meander at will, causing her to grit her teeth in frustration on occasion, even though they had all agreed the time lost was worth the gain in secrecy. And on top of it all, a cold rain had started the day before, adding a chilly dampness to the air that made her pull her heavy black cloak even tighter around her willowy form.

She peered out into the darkness and wondered how far it was to the next inn. How she longed for a hot cup of tea and just a few hours of uninterrupted sleep. . . . The coach hit a particularly nasty rut, knocking her back against the worn squabs and drawing a loud oath from John Coachman. A pang of guilt shot through her and she chastised herself for dwelling on her own discomforts, compared to what her servants were suffering. Last night, Polly had developed a bad fever, and though she tried to disguise it, by morning she was in a bad enough state that Caroline had insisted that she be left behind at a small inn.

Despite his mutterings, John Coachman couldn't disagree when he saw the girl's wan face and felt her burning brow. By the time a room had been procured, along with the innkeeper's promise to send for a doctor once he had been paid in advance for a week's lodging, more hours had slipped by. Caroline wouldn't hear of continuing until she had seen the girl comfortably settled and provided with enough funds to take a coach back to Roxbury Manor. At least John had been able to grab some rest.

But now he seemed determined to make up for lost time. On they drove, though the night was so black Caroline wondered at how he kept the horses on the road. The thick, scudding clouds only let through a pale wash of moonlight on occasion, and the wind, which had whistled down upon them from the bleak moor during the past hour, promised more rain. She could only imagine what miseries poor John was enduring in such conditions. She sighed, wedging into a corner and bracing herself with her shoulder to counter the increasingly heavy jolts.

Her thoughts couldn't help but turn to the enormity of what she had undertaken. The lives of many brave people depended on her ability to succeed, and that made the mission daunting enough. But if she were truly honest with herself, that was not the only reason she had chosen to embark on such a hazardous course. Oh, it was true enough what she had told Darwin—that she would never have asked a servant to risk his life. But there had been other choices. No doubt she would have been commended for showing good sense had she appealed to her father's close friend and neighbor, Lord Ellsworth, for advice.

Caroline's lips quirked in an involuntary smile. Eminent good sense was not a trait normally associated with her name. Perhaps that was because she had spent too much time racketing around with her cousin Lucien—she, the younger, always pushing herself to match his exploits.

Or perhaps it was because of something else.

Lucien was part of it, to be sure. Both her mother and his parents had died during a particularly bad influenza epidemic, and so he had come to live under her father's roof. Aside from the fact that the Duke doted on his young nephew, it was only natural that he do so—after all, Lucien was the heir. And so the two of them had become like brother and sister, both being close in age and having no true siblings of their own. He had tolerated her following him around like an eager puppy when they were small, and as they grew older, he had never sought to keep her from taking part in his escapades because of the mere fact of her being female. From filching apples from Squire Laidlaw's trees to racing curricles at midnight down the fashionable streets of Mayfair, Lucien had always treated her as an equal.

Yet Caroline always knew, from her earliest days, it was not so. No matter that she had a better seat on her hunter than most of the county or could discuss estate affairs with enough knowledge to set a lax steward's ears to ringing. No matter that she could read Virgil or Homer in the original or discuss the political implications of Napoleon's return to France with more acuity than half of White's. She would never be her father's heir. His beloved Roxbury would not pass on to one of his own flesh and blood, and that must be a terrible disappointment to him. Her hand came up to brush away from her cheek what must have been an errant drop of rain. This once, however, she would prove to everyone that despite what Society decreed, she was worthy of her family name. A sigh caught in her throat—if only she could prove it to the one who mattered most.

She must have dozed off, for she was jolted awake by the sound of a sharp crack. Still muzzy from fatigue, she thought perhaps she had imagined it. But suddenly there was another one, and she sat bolt upright, for there was no mistaking the sound of gunfire. At the same time, the coach picked up speed, rocking wildly from side to side. Caroline was thrown violently against the door.

"John!" she cried. "John! What is happening?"

There was no answer over the pounding of the hooves and the groaning of the wooden joints.

Frantically, she pried at the door's handle, opening it enough to peer out towards the rear. Two dark shapes, blacker than the night, were charging down on them. A brief flash was followed by the bark of a pistol. After that, the coach seemed to gain even more speed. Caroline twisted her head towards the front but couldn't see up to the box. The moon broke through the clouds for a moment. From her angle, she could see the horses were out of control. Panicked, they galloped madly ahead, the reins dragging helplessly through the mud and ruts. The front wheels gave a dizzying lurch as the coach left the road, careening over rougher terrain. Ahead was . . . nothing. Nothing but an ominous black void. Caroline had only seconds to make a decision.

She flung herself out the door.

A searing pain shot through her shoulder as she hit the ground hard. The breath was knocked out of her and the momentum of the fall sent her tumbling down a steep slope. Her head grazed an outcropping of rock, opening up a jagged gash across her brow. Though half dazed, the sound of splintering wood and the terrified whinnies of the horses filled her ears. And she couldn't seem to stop rolling, sliding, tumbling over more rocks and brush as brambles tore at her clothes.

Finally, her descent was arrested by a large gorse bush. Wedged among its thorny lower branches, Caroline was barely conscious. She groaned aloud at the thought of poor John—the past few minutes had been a nightmare worse than anything Dante could have penned. She tried to sit up, but the slightest movement caused her to retch. Falling back, face-down in the mud and leaves, she lay motionless.

Above her, the sound of pounding hooves stopped abruptly. Through the haze of shock, she could hear other sounds, the sounds of boots scrabbling over rocks, and then the sounds of voices.

"Ain't bloody likely a living thing survived that," came a rough growl.

"Cor, watcha gone and done by popping off the coachman? We 'us supposed te git some piece of paper from the wench afore we killed 'um." The second voice had a grating whine to it.

There was a loud grunt. "Let's be off and collect the rest of our blunt from that flash cove—don't like the looks of 'im by half. He's as like to scamper on us, if I knows that type."

"But whadda we tell him?"

"Ye ninny. We tell him she's dead, that's wot. And that's what he bloody hired us fer, ain't it?"

"He seemed mighty particular about wanting that letter she had."

The first voice swore. "You wanna go down there and git it fer him?"

There was a silence.

"Didn't think so," continued the voice. "The gennulmun be welcome to break his own arse if it's so important te him."

"Who was she, anyhow?"

"Who bloody cares. Whoever she be, she's dead. Let's be off."

Caroline didn't hear them leave. She had slipped into a blackness as deep as the starless sky.

"How long before the mill can be working?"

The steward pulled a face as he rubbed at his chin. "Assuming we have the mortar and timber, and enough men can be pulled from the other work . . ." He let the words trail off as he stared at the forlorn stone structure which was in an obvious state of disrepair.

Julian Fitzwilliam Atherton, the new Earl of Davenport, sighed. "Figure out a cost for that, too."

The other man scratched something in a worn notebook and then they both spurred their horses forward and continued along the riverbank. They rode in silence for a while, each man seemingly occupied with his own thoughts.

"Perhaps you should hand the bloody place over to the creditors and be done with it," murmured the steward as they passed yet another field fallow for lack of seed.

The Earl's jaw tightened. "I am not intimidated by a difficult task, Sykes. Things will be different now."

Sykes shot him an appraising glance. "Aye, milord, on that I have no doubt—you ain't like him at all." He heaved a sigh. "Well, if you're serious, the tenants will most likely come around. They are good folk and not afraid of hard work. Perhaps it won't be impossible to set things right."

Davenport nodded grimly. "Bring your list tomorrow morning at nine and we shall decide where to begin." With that, he turned his mount away from the other man and set the big black stallion into a canter towards home.

He loosened the cravat at his neck as he strode from the stable to the main house. His shirt was damp with sweat and his worn riding coat showed the effects of a day spent in the saddle. He glanced ruefully at the mud encrusting his boots—hardly the picture of a titled gentleman, he thought to himself with an ironic smile. But he cared little for appearances. His mind was already occupied with the myriad things that needed to be done. First, he must pen a letter to his banker in London. His own carefully managed funds should be sufficient to satisfy the most pressing demands of his creditors and still leave enough to begin to put things right. With prudent management, hard work and luck . . .

The front door was opened by a rotund man of less than average height. His wiry hair seemed to defy all efforts with a brush, sticking straight up from his head as if he had recently encountered a castle ghost. That, combined with his rather large eyes and pinched mouth, gave him a perpetually startled look. But at least, noted Davenport, there was no longer a stab of fear in the other man's eyes every time he approached.

"Good evening, Owens," said the Earl.

The butler bowed, lower than was necessary. He was still having trouble finding his tongue. "G-g-good evening, my lord," he finally stammered. "Y-you have a visitor."

The Earl sighed and ran a hand through his dark, tousled locks. He hadn't bothered with a hat, and his hair, worn longer than was fashionable, was as dusty as the rest of him.

"Who is it?" he inquired.

"L-lady Atherton, my lord. I put her in th-the library."

"I trust you lit the fire."

The man nodded.

"Very well." He let out another sigh. At the moment, he didn't feel nearly up to facing his brother's widow—what he really wanted was a hot bath and a bottle of brandy. But it must be done.

He opened the library door.

"Hello, Julian." She was still as lovely as when he had

first met her, though her mouth seemed harder, more care-worn, and her eyes were perhaps a shade duller. "I apologize for coming unannounced."

"You are always welcome here, Helen."

She smiled fleetingly. "You are . . . too good."

Davenport crossed to the mahogany sideboard and poured himself a generous brandy. "May I get you anything?" he asked, gesturing to the sherry.

She shook her head, her gaze dropping to her hands, which lay knotted in her lap.

He stared into the fire and took a long swallow from his glass.

"Actually, I've come to say good-bye."

His head jerked around with a start.

"I have a small property in New Forest, near Lymington, and a modest income to go with it. It came to me through my mother and was one thing Charles could not touch." She paused, trying to control the emotion in her voice.

"You may always think of this as your home," he said quietly. "The dower house can be refurbished . . ."

"No!" she cried. "This was never my home, God knows. And I am a reminder of—you have borne more than any man should have to bear." Her voice broke. "The lies, the ugly rumors that have been bandied about your name. Don't think I am unaware of what I owe you!"

"It isn't necessary . . ."

"Yes! Yes, it is. Julian please let me say it aloud. It is only your willingness to take the blame for many of Charles's . . . excesses that allows me to appear in Society without being cut directly by all my acquaintances, that allows my daughter to grow up without hanging her head in total shame—"

"Helen."

Tears were gathering in her eyes. "I'm glad I never bore him a son," she whispered. "I'm glad Highwood went to you, who deserves it so much more than any seed of Charles's—though God knows, there are probably more than enough of those in the area."

"Helen," he repeated quietly. "Don't do this to yourself."

She struggled to compose herself. "Lord, what an utter fool I was, Julian."

"Aren't we all?"

"How could I have been so blind? And how can you have ever forgiven me?"

"It was a long time ago," he said gently. "And we all know how charming Charles could be when he wanted to be."

She shook her head. "How can two people so alike on the outside be so different on the inside?"

Davenport ran a finger along the thin white line that marred his cheekbone. "Ah," he said, his voice full of self-mockery. "Not alike—I'm the twin with the scar."

Lady Helen regarded him with a look of great sorrow, and some other emotion.

He turned to look out the large, leaded glass windows.

She continued to stare at his tall, athletic form even though his back was to her. "What of you, Julian? Well I know that Charles has mortgaged the estate to the hilt and gambled away any money that your father didn't lose before him."

"I shall manage."

A sigh escaped her lips. "It looks to be turning into a nasty night." She had risen and moved to stand by his side. "I shall take my leave so that I may return to my uncle's before the rain begins." Placing a slender hand on his shoulder she stood on tiptoes to brush a kiss on his cheek.

"Would that the hands of time could be turned back," she whispered.

He shook his head bleakly. "That, I fear, is beyond the power of any mortal."

She smiled sadly and looked as if to say more. Then her lips pressed together, and after a moment's hesitation, she simply sighed.

"Good-bye then, Julian. I wish you all the happiness you deserve." Without waiting for a response, she hurried from the room.

"Happiness. That, I fear, is beyond my power as well," he whispered to himself.

Then he poured himself another brandy.

Would that the spirits could wash away the bitter taste that stuck in his throat, no matter how much of the amber liquid he poured into himself. It brought only oblivion, not sweet relief from the sea of demands that washed over him. He was heartily sick of it, sick of feeling that slowly, inexorably, he was losing a little piece of himself with every crashing wave.

With a grimace he realized he hardly remembered how it had all started. When had his mother first opportuned him to have a care for his twin, to try to temper the high spirits of the heir and guard both him and the family name from harm. Why, he and his brother could not have been above ten or twelve years of age, but even then, Charles had been irresistibly charming, while he had been painfully dull.

And dim-witted as well, to allow himself to become his brother's keeper. The pattern had been set then. Charles became increasingly wild while he was left to quietly make amends for his sibling's excesses or take the blame himself. Sometimes it was just easier that way. It had made his father laugh and his mother cry. He supposed it was those anguished eyes that had kept him from shirking from the unfair responsibilities. She had cared about family honor and right and wrong. His own principles must have come from her side of the family, for as much as he wished to, he could not simply walk away.

And that was just the beginning. Much as his mind rebelled against it, he forced himself to think about Helen. Charles had not been content with merely stealing his good name—no, his brother had to take the woman he loved as well. Davenport paused to drain his glass.

Charming Charles.

His brother had been free and easy with his addresses while he, Davenport, was shy and awkward. How could he blame a lovely young lady for being seduced by well-turned phrases and elegant manners.

Unfortunately, when in his cups, his brother became as free and easy with his fists as with his pretty words. Davenport's face darkened as he recalled his first sight of the bruises. She had begged him not to make a scene. So, once again, he had dutifully done what was asked of him, no matter the cost to his own feelings. Had Helen truly any notion of what torture it had been to watch what was happening to her? His own suffering must surely have been nearly as painful as hers.

His fingers came up to trace the thin white scar on his cheekbone as his jaw tightened in anger. Rather than stand up for herself, Helen had turned to him for comfort. How unfair a burden! Why was it he fell prey to vulnerable females? He found himself wondering, not for the first time, what it would be like to care for someone capable of giving as well as taking.

Well, his brother was dead now, and he intended to bury his own past weaknesses along with him. He meant to finally get on with his own life.

But first he would uncork another bottle.

Caroline had no notion of how long she had been lying there. It was still pitch black and the rain had begun anew, light, intermittent drops, but chilling to the bone. She pushed herself into a sitting position, fighting down a new wave of nausea. The pain in her left arm was excruciating.

She couldn't move it, but with her right one she assured herself that the small packet sewn into the fold of her dress was still there. The feel of it triggered the memory of the conversation she had heard between her assailants. It seemed so unreal, but then her fingers moved up to her bruised face, sticky with blood.

She knew she had to move from where she was. With daylight, there was a good chance they might return. Summoning up all her strength, she crawled out from the gorse and made her way on hands and knees back up to the road. Using a tree for support, she pulled herself to her feet, clutching her muddy cloak tightly around her aching body. Thankfully, the rain let up once again. Clouds scudded across the sky to reveal a pale moon. Her eyes could follow the road around a sharp bend to where it disappeared into a forest of live oak and beeches. But she quickly decided against such a course. The steep ravine fell away to the right. There was really little choice. On the other side of the road was a field, then a copse of trees. With faltering steps, she headed for their shelter.

It was a larger woods than she had thought. Though thankful for the cover, she found it difficult to pick her way through the tangle of brush and brambles. One step at a time, she repeated to herself. Then another, and another. She forced herself to keep moving. Only once, on crossing a small stream, did she allow herself to stop for a moment. The water felt cool and comforting as she drank thirstily and washed the worst of the dirt and dried blood from her face. The urge to lie down was overwhelming, but she forced herself back to her feet.

She had to keep going.

Daylight began to tint the horizon. Caroline was out of the trees and had passed through a number of fields overgrown with weeds and wild blackberry bushes. Now she found herself on some sort of path. Birds began chirping as the light became stronger. A fox darted out in front of her, returning to its den from a nocturnal hunting foray. Startled, she stopped dead in her tracks, then chided herself for being so skittish. Just a little farther, she promised herself, but somehow her feet would not seem to obey her commands any longer. Swaying slightly, she crumpled to the ground.

Chapter Two

Davenport winced as the light struck his face. He turned to escape the piercing rays, and groaned at the dull throbbing at his temples. Then it occurred to him that the sun never came into his bedchamber in such a manner. One eye reluctantly pried open. It took in the carved fireplace, now cold with grey ashes, the oak bookcases. . . .

That explained it. He had never made it to his bed last night. He grimaced as he struggled into a sitting position. The couch had been deucedly uncomfortable on his back, but that part of his anatomy didn't ache nearly as much as his head. He spied two empty bottles on the rug and a third one, nearly gone, on the table next to the stump of a candle. He swung his feet to the carpet. Good Lord, he hadn't even removed his muddy boots.

Raking his hands through his tangled hair, he glanced at the tall case clock on the mantel. It was barely five-thirty in the morning. Sykes was to arrive at nine. He brushed the palm of his hand over the rough stubble on his chin—he must look as terrible as he felt! A breath of fresh air would no doubt help to clear his head. There would be plenty of time for a bath and a shave.

He rose, a trifle unsteady, and pulled on his coat. At least he had thought to remove that garment and it looked marginally better than the rest of him. No matter. There would be not a soul abroad to take in his shocking state of dishevelment at this hour, not along the path he intended to ride.

The wind did indeed feel good against his face, though his horse's spirited gallop caused his queasy stomach a lurch or two. He slowed the big stallion into an easy walk, though the animal tossed his head in disgust at being denied his usual distance.

"Easy, Nero," he said, patting the glistening neck. "I promise to give you your head later today."

The horse snorted in reply, then suddenly shied to one side.

Davenport let out an oath as his stomach gave an unpleasant heave. "Behave yourself," he grumbled, tightening the reins.

The horse pranced back, and suddenly Davenport could see what was making him behave so skittishly.

"Good God," he exclaimed as he quickly dismounted and knelt by the body lying in the middle of the muddy path. He gently turned the person over and placed a finger on the side of the neck. There was a pulse, so she—it was a female, he had noted—was alive, but she looked in far worse shape than he did.

Caroline gave a low moan and her eyes fluttered open. Not six inches from her face was another face, a man's face. The eyes were bloodshot, a black stubble bristled on his jaw and raven hair fell wildly to the shoulders of a worn coat. The odor of brandy was quite apparent.

She gave a yelp and let fly with her good hand.

"Ouch!"

Davenport fell back on his rump, nursing a tender nose. A trickle of blood started from one nostril. He fished out a rumpled handkerchief from his coat pocket and pressed it to the injured appendage.

"Who the hell taught you to throw a punch like that?" he demanded in a muffled voice as he righted himself but stayed out of arm's reach.

There was no answer.

"If you are bamming me and mean to plant me another facer, I'll not be pleased," he warned as he inched closer. "I'm merely trying to be a gentleman and offer some assistance."

Her eyes were closed and she didn't move.

Davenport took in the darkening bruises, the scratches and the nasty cut on her forehead and his lips tightened. "I wonder what brute it is you are trying to flee," he muttered as he gathered her in his arms and remounted his horse.

The day, which had started badly enough, seemed to be getting much worse.

"There it be, down there. See?"

The elegantly dressed gentleman craned his neck to peer down into the ravine.

"Ain't nubbody gonna walk away from that," piped up the third man as he shifted his weight nervously from side to side.

The gentleman said nothing. He stepped off the ledge and picked his way a short distance down the overgrown slope, stopping to steady himself against a scraggly birch tree.

"Ain't nubbody gonna notice them down there neither, leastways not for months." The man who had spoken first wet his lips. "Yer gonna give us the rest of the blunt now, ain't ye? They're dead, and that's what ye said ye wanted."

The gentleman scrambled back up to the road. He reached into his voluminous cape and withdrew a heavy leather pouch, which he tossed at the feet of the two other men. They fell to their knees in their eagerness to retrieve it, nearly knocking heads. But their hands froze as two quick shots rang out. Slowly, each pitched forward into the mud.

"You are right—no one will see the bodies for months," he repeated softly as he tucked two long-barreled pistols back into his pockets.

Removing his cape, he dragged each body over the edge of the ravine and sent them tumbling down into the underbrush. Satisfied that nothing suspicious was visible from the road, he brushed some smudges of mud from his clothes with a grimace of distaste and retrieved his outer garment. He knew a nearby ostler who would be happy to handle the sale of two horses, no questions asked. Then he could return and take a closer look down in the ravine. The girl might be dead, as the two highwaymen claimed, but they had badly bungled the job.

The dispatch.

He had risked too much to see it slip out of his grasp. He would have it, no matter what.

This time, when Caroline opened her eyes, the face she saw was not nearly so disreputable-looking. The eyes were not bloodshot at all, but a clear hazel, narrowed with concern. A full beard, flecked liberally with grey, obscured the other features, save for a long, hooked nose.

"She is awake." The face turned to speak to someone else in the room.

Caroline vaguely recalled being taught by her governess how many bones were in the human body. It was quite a number, and every single one of hers seemed to hurt abominably. At least, she noted, she was no longer lying on hard ground but in a blessedly soft bed, with an eiderdown coverlet pulled up over her. Then, as she became more fully conscious, the memories of the past few days came flooding back.

"My clothes!" She tried to raise her head, but fell back with a gasp.

"Easy now, miss." The face had turned back to her. "Don't try to move. You've taken a nasty blow to the head."

She tried to sit up again but someone gently held her shoulder down.

"There is no need to be alarmed, miss. Your dress and, er, other garments are right here. Mrs. Collins has placed them over a chair to dry."

"Who are you?" she demanded.

"I am Dr. Laskins—"

Another voice cut off the doctor. "The more appropriate question is who are *you*?"

Caroline couldn't see the speaker. She ignored the question. "How did I get here? The last thing I remember is being accosted by some ruffian. I fought him off . . ."

There was a low chuckle. "Indeed, Laskins is treating two patients this morning. His verdict is that I shall survive. Your condition is causing him a bit more concern."

The eyes were no longer bloodshot, which only emphasized the startling depth of their sapphire color. The cheeks were freshly shaven, revealing a lean, strong jaw and chin whose squareness was broken only by a slight cleft in the middle. The chiseled lips were curved in a hint of a smile. Though not nearly as close as the last time, it was indeed the same face—Caroline recognized the small hairline scar running along the cheekbone, the only subtle flaw in an otherwise dashingly handsome visage.

"I'm Davenport. Let me inquire once again—who are you?"

Caroline closed her eyes. She resolved to say nothing until she had time to think more clearly.

"My lord, the young lady has suffered a severe blow to the head. Let us not tax her until she feels strong enough to speak. The important thing is for her to rest. The laudanum will soon be taking effect and that should dull the pain she must be in."

Caroline did feel a pleasant wooziness creeping over her. Stay mum, she urged herself. But she couldn't help it. One eye flicked open, taking in the gentleman's rough flaxen shirt and worn jacket. "A *lord*," she mumbled. "You must be joking. Looks more like a . . . a farmhand."

Davenport gave a short laugh. "You have the right of it there, my mysterious stranger. I'm nought but a farmer. Which reminds me, I have a meeting with my steward. So, as you advise, Laskins, we will postpone any further questions until later."

Dr. Laskins closed his portmanteau. "I shall return this afternoon. She should be more alert by then."

Caroline certainly hoped so. She needed all her wits about her to decide what to do next.

The Duke of Cheviot paced up and down beside the command tent, heedless of the thick mud that was starting to work its way up his tall Hessians. In the distance, the dull thuds of cannon fire reverberated in the hills. A military aide rushed out of the tent, quickly mounted a big chestnut stallion and urged the animal into a full gallop. He was followed by an older gentleman whose bearing as well as his uniform marked him as the one in command.

"General . . ." began the Duke.

"I'm sorry, Your Grace. Your group must move out with us. The lines to the north have been cut off."

"But I must be in London! It is of the utmost urgency, I assure you!"

The general shook his head. "Not possible. We must move immediately."

"Perhaps with an escort? The lives of many of our men may depend on it."

The general frowned. "I tell you, it's too risky. I do not know your exact mission, Your Grace, but I do know that Whitehall depends on me to see to *your* life. Besides, there are no men to spare. Perhaps in a few days, if we are lucky."

The Duke clenched his hands. "At least may I send a letter through?"

The general gazed into the distance, his eyes riveted on the thin red lines moving through a ruined cornfield. "Nothing but military dispatches," he snapped. "Can't you see what is happening here? Gather the others and be ready to move in ten minutes."

It was quite clear which rank took precedence on the battlefield.

Davenport rubbed his temples. Good Lord, it was a lot of money, but he could manage it, just barely. He smiled in grim humor at the last remark of the young lady upstairs—there would be no new wardrobe from Weston or boots from Hoby, that was for sure. Not that it mattered. He had no intention of venturing to Town anytime soon. He had meant what he had said about being a farmer. It was time someone of his lineage set the estate to rights.

With that in mind, he closed the ledger book and reached for his jacket. The feel of the coarse wool made him smile again. He did have clothes befitting a gentleman, but these garments were more practical, given that he intended to work alongside his tenants. As well as keeping his mind occupied, it would show them the new Earl was not at all like his older brother, no matter what it appeared.

But it was a sharp observation the stranger had made. Davenport's brow furrowed as he walked to the stable. Who was she, and how had she received such cuts and bruises? He could swear he had seen a look of wariness cross her face for an instant when he had asked her who she was. In fact, he was sure she had deliberately avoided answering his question. His lips compressed. He had seen similar injuries on the face of a lady. It sickened him, but he told himself in this case, it was none of his business. He planned to get her back to whoever was responsible for her as soon as possible. Another helpless female was the last sort of distraction he needed in his life.

Sykes was waiting for him, holding the reins of the big black stallion, who was tossing his head even more impatiently than earlier in the morning. Davenport patted the muscular neck.

"You shall have your run before the day is out, Nero," he promised as he swung into the saddle. But he kept the horse in tight check as the two men headed out to the fields. There was still much to discuss concerning work to be done.

They approached an expanse of fallow land. A group of men, stripped to the waist and already covered with a film of dust, were toiling to clear the overgrown weeds from the soil.

"I went ahead and purchased seed. There is still time to get a crop in if we hurry," said Sykes.

The men looked up as the two riders slowed their pace. Some nodded a curt greeting to the steward while most simply stood and regarded the Earl with suspicion.

"You have your work cut out for you, milord," observed Sykes in a low voice as they dismounted.

Davenport nodded grimly and began to remove his shirt.

The horse's flanks were lathered with sweat. Even though he was bone-tired, Davenport had enjoyed the hard gallop back to the manor house. The cool breeze felt good on his parched skin and blew some of the dust from his hair. It was brutally hard work, but so far he had not disgraced himself. He stripped to no disadvantage with his broad shoulders and lithe build. And though the surreptitious glances cast his way throughout the day seemed to expect—nay, wish for—his collapse, he had accomplished as much as any man there. They might not like him yet, he thought with satisfaction, but they were a fair way along to respecting him. That was what Sykes had told him—that he would have to earn their trust.

That was fair enough, as long as they gave him a fighting chance.

The doctor's gig stood by the stable as he rode in. Davenport swore under his breath. He had forgotten all about his mysterious visitor. Tossing the reins to the grizzled groom who shuffled out from the stalls, he strode quickly to the main house and barely gave Owens a chance to yank the door open for him. He was about to continue up the staircase when he paused for a moment and asked the butler for hot water to be brought up to his chamber. For some reason, he found himself wanting to wash the worst of the dirt from his person and put on a clean shirt before he looked in on the girl. A mere farmer was fine, but he balked at appearing a complete yokel, especially after the rather unfortunate first impression he had made.

The door to the room was slightly ajar. Dr. Laskins was already finishing a cursory examination. The young lady's face, its pallor emphasized by the white bandage around her forehead, showed some deep scratches across the cheeks and bruises near the eyes that were already mottling into an ugly purplish hue. Despite the injuries, it was an intriguing face. He had already noted the emerald eyes, now closed in repose. The nose was classically straight though perhaps a bit too long. High cheekbones stood out as a dominant feature while the mouth, rather wider than was thought pretty in a lady, was full and firm, even now set in a look of determination. An unusual face, oddly attractive. Masses of honey-colored hair tumbled around it, spreading out over the pillow. The earl found himself wondering if it felt as silky as it looked. . . .

He turned his gaze quickly to Laskins. "How is your patient this evening?"

The doctor regarded him over lowered spectacle. "She seems to be resting comfortably, a good sign. I am loath to disturb her sleep, so I shall leave a draught of laudanum and ask Mrs. Collins to look in occasionally during the night." He looked down at her sleeping form. "As I told you earlier, my examination revealed no broken bones, but the shoulder—the joint must be set back in place."

Davenport frowned.

"Aye, it will be quite painful, but there's no getting around it. I shall wait until she seems a little stronger."

"Wouldn't it be better to do it now, when she is unconscious?"

Dr. Laskins shook his head. "I dare not risk it. The shock to the system might be too great."

Davenport's frown deepened. "Any idea who she is?"

The doctor shook his head again. "I have made a few discreet inquiries, but there's no talk of a missing girl from this area. I wonder . . ." He let his voice trail off. "It is clear she is gently bred, for her hands show little sign of manual work. Whoever she is, she has had a rough time of it lately."

"Has she been beaten?"

"It is hard to tell. There are bruises on her body, but it is impossible to tell for sure what caused them. If it is a father or a husband, he is a brute."

The Earl's teeth set on edge as he remembered how Helen had looked once when he had arrived on an unexpected visit.

"I shall return in the morning," continued the other man. "I don't expect there to be any problems during the night, but if she wakes, Mrs. Collins should try to get her to take some nourishment."

Davenport walked the doctor to the door and, with one last glance at the sleeping patient, shut it softly.

Caroline waited a few minutes to make sure they were truly gone, then slowly opened her eyes. Her head and shoulder ached like the devil, but the laudanum had dulled some of the pain and the sleep had at least allowed her to marshal her thoughts. She looked around. It was a pleasant room, plain but light and airy. From a window to her left, the sun cast its sinking rays onto the oak floor, warming it to a soft, honeyed color. The simple bed was more than comfortable and as she settled herself deeper into its thick softness she decided that, for the moment, she seemed safe enough.

But for how long?

She had seen her host's expression this morning. He would not be put off much longer before his questions began again. And despite his rough appearance and shabby dress, he did not appear to be a slowtop. No, there was a depth to those sapphire eyes that warned her he would not be fooled by any shallow Banbury tale.

Caroline heaved a small sigh. So what, exactly, could she tell him? As she mentally recounted the actual events of the past few days she realized that even to herself they sounded more gothic than a Radcliffe novel, especially since she dared not offer an explanation. The information she carried was vital to England's war effort. She would trust no one with her secret. She wouldn't let her country—or her father—down. If only he had given her a clearer picture of the dangers.

Drat it! If she had been a man, if she . . .

The look in her eyes, smudged with pain and weariness as they were, would have warned anyone who knew her well that she was roused for battle. She was just as clever as Papa and Lucien, she told herself. And certainly more so than dear Uncle Henry, who would be utterly at a loss as to how to deal with a conundrum whose origins were less than a century old. Put her faith in someone who barely managed to remember to leave the sanctuary of his library for meals? She thought not. Despite her father's orders, Uncle

Henry would be the last person she would look to for help. She was going to have to rely on herself.

She thought for a moment on the snatches of conversation she had just overheard. From what she could gather, it seemed they thought she was fleeing a husband who beat her. Her lips pursed. Lucien had once told her that if one was going to tell a hum, it was best to base it as much as possible on the truth. At least this saved her from having to concoct a credible story of her own. Perhaps it was best to leave that impression for the moment.

The rider reined in the grey stallion and looked around carefully, assuring himself that no one was about to note his presence. He dismounted and led his horse off the road into a thick copse of beech trees. His mouth tightened in distaste as he surveyed the steepness of the ravine, the rocks, the brush, the mud and his own immaculately polished Hessians. It had to be done, nonetheless. The descent was difficult, but the gentleman, though of only average height, was powerfully built and negotiated the treacherous footing with a certain lithe grace.

The carriage lay shattered, half submerged in the river that cut through the tumbled boulders and granite outcroppings. Amid the twisted wreckage lay the bloodied carcasses of the horses which were already beginning to swell and attract flies. The coachman's body lay face-down near a broken wheel. With the toe of his boot, the gentleman turned the dead man over. The bullet wound at the base of the neck explained the other carnage. With a muttered oath at the stupidity of the hired ruffians, the gentleman let the disfigured face fall back in the mud. They truly had made things more difficult than necessary. He picked his way to where the door of the carriage hung precariously by one hinge. Wresting it open, he peered inside.

There was nothing but a small valise.

He stood motionless for a few moments, as if in deep thought. His hand reached in and fished it out. It didn't take long to search it and its contents thoroughly. He tossed it aside, his grim expression showing no surprise at not finding what he was looking for. Then with slow, deliberate steps he walked a way along the river until a pile of boulders blocked any further progress. There was no sign of a body. His eyes gauged the current. Yes, it was possible. It could have been carried downstream.

With another oath, the gentleman turned and began to trace his steps back up to the road. He dared not linger in the spot too long. Damn the chit, he cursed to himself. She had to be dead, she *had* to be! Her body should be there. And so should the papers. He paused and looked back down the slope. Nothing could survive a fall over that. As he grabbed a small sapling to steady his climb, his eyes fell to a nearby gorse bush, not far from the crest in the road. Clinging to one of its thorny branches was a small strip of dark cloth.

Davenport ran his hands through his hair. His long legs were stretched out towards the meager fire and an open book lay on his lap. Good Lord, he thought, he needn't resort to brandy to help him sleep. He had only to essay a few chapters on the raising of sheep—though the pages on breeding had reminded him how uncomfortably long it had been since he had enjoyed the pleasures of the opposite sex. A sigh escaped his lips. Well, like many other things, that would just have to wait until he could visit Town. He had no intention of taking on his brother's habits as well as his title.

He closed the book with more force than necessary. At least his body felt pleasantly tired from the physical exertion of the day's labor. He wouldn't need to rely on the effects of brandy or boring tomes to help him get some rest tonight. Taking up his candle, he rose and set off for his bedchamber. It was quite late. The house was in total darkness, save for his solitary light, as the Earl climbed the wide staircase and made his way quietly down the corridor. At the door to the mysterious stranger's room, he paused, then opened it and entered.

In sleep, her face had softened, easing the edge of wariness he had noticed that morning. She looked even younger, more vulnerable. His mouth quirked in a slight smile as he recalled the shot she had landed on his nose. She had spunk, whoever she was. The smile dissolved into a slight frown. He hoped the matter of her identity and her situation would prove simple, but somehow, in the pit of his stomach, he sensed that nothing about her was simple.

He had a problem on his hands, and that was the last thing he needed.

Caroline awoke with sunlight streaming over her face. It felt warm and—pain shot through her shoulder as she turned towards the window, bringing her sharply back to reality. She sat up as best she could, once again aware that she was in a strange room, in a strange house, on a strange mission. Her stomach rumbled loudly, reminding her that she had not eaten in more than twenty-four hours. In fact, she was famished. She was contemplating just how much longer she could hold out when salvation, in the massive form of Mrs. Collins, pushed open the door, arms laden with a large tray from which emanated the most heavenly smells.

"I brought ye some porridge and a pot of tea," announced the older woman upon noticing that Caroline was awake. "Ye must be starving, ye poor thing."

Caroline made a squeak.

The housekeeper put the tray down and settled her ample backside on the side of the bed. "Here now, let me help ye."

She spooned up a large helping and guided it towards Caroline's mouth.

As the steaming mixture of oats, thick cream and sugar slid down her throat, Caroline's eyes closed in bliss.

Mrs. Collins nodded in approval. "Need to put some meat on them bones," she remarked as she thrust forward another bite.

It didn't take long for the bowl to be emptied.

"Thank you." Caroline gave the woman a smile of gratitude. She felt much better. "That was wonderful."

The woman held a cup of tea to Caroline's lips. "That nasty knock on the head ain't affected yer appetite, it seems. I'll bring more, as soon as the doctor says it is all right." She surveyed what little of Caroline showed from beneath the bedcovers. "At least yer a sight more comfortable than ye was when his lordship dragged ye in here." Her eyes shifted to the muddy garments over the chair. "Shall I try to mend those?" she asked, though her expression showed what she thought of the effort. "Or perhaps I should . . ."

"No!" cried Caroline. "I mean—thank you, but please, just leave them. I am quite skillful with a needle."

The housekeeper merely shrugged her shoulders.

Once again Caroline was aware of the delicate lace at her neck. "Whose is this?" she inquired, her eyes falling to the fine lawn material.

"Oh, that's an old one of Lady Atherton's. Lucky the two of you are close to the same size, though yer a mite taller."

Caroline's eyes narrowed with interest. "His lordship"— she tried to remember his name—"is married, then?"

At that moment, the doctor walked in, followed by Davenport. "I see our patient is awake this morning and able to take a little sustenance." He nodded in approval at the empty bowl. "Nothing more than gruel today, then tomorrow maybe I shall allow something more substantial."

Caroline's stomach growled in protest.

Mrs. Collins cleared the tray, making room for Dr. Laskins at the side of the bed. He felt Caroline's forehead, then took gentle hold of her wrist.

"No sign of fever," he said. "And the pulse feels strong. You have a good constitution, young lady, to have weathered the ordeal you have been through with no further ill effects." His hand moved to Caroline's shoulder. The mere touch made her wince.

The doctor's expression turned to one of concern. "However, we are going to have to deal with that injury. The shoulder has come out of its socket. It must be set back."

Caroline closed her eyes. She had seen such a thing happen to a groom at Roxbury Manor. She could still remember his screams as three men had wrestled to pop the offending limb back into place.

Davenport spoke for the first time. "Is there no alternative?"

The doctor shook his head. "It must be done. Perhaps a footman might come up and assist me?"

Davenport pulled a face. "I have no footmen. I shall lend a hand—but wait." He left the room and returned in a few minutes with a large tumbler filled with amber liquid.

"Drink this," he ordered.

Caroline looked at him in consternation. "Wha—"

As soon as she opened her mouth, the Earl grasped her jaw and unceremoniously dumped the entire contents of the glass down her throat.

Caroline sputtered wildly, sending a spray of tiny droplets over the front of Davenport's shirt. "That . . . that was extremely unnecessary. You needn't have forced me!"

"I have little time to argue," he countered.

"You are no gentleman." She glowered at him.

"So I have been told on numerous occasions," he muttered.

"What was that foul . . ." Caroline sniffed the air, then shot the Earl a scathing look. "Do you always reek of brandy?"

"Only when driven to it by difficult females," he answered through clenched teeth. He looked down at his soiled shirt in dismay. Damnation, he would have to change, else his men think he was no different than the previous Earl. And that was his last clean shirt. He glared back at the girl, then turned his gaze to the doctor. "A few more minutes and we should be able to begin."

The doctor smiled grimly and folded his arms across his chest.

"What do you mean?" asked Caroline

Davenport ignored her question and began to converse with the other man about the weather, the state of Squire Dawson's broken leg and the price of wheat as if she wasn't there.

Caroline felt a rush of anger. At least, it must be that, for she felt hot all over. It was strange, however. In the past, even when she had really lost her temper, she had never felt so . . . odd. She narrowed her eyes, for it was becoming increasing difficult to focus.

All of a sudden she giggled. "Stop swaying! You are making me dizzy," she said to the Earl, though it was her own head that was lolling from side to side.

The doctor rolled up his sleeves. "I think we may begin."

"I feel terrible," announced Caroline, her speech slightly slurred.

"You are about to feel worse," replied Davenport as he took hold of her good arm.

The doctor grasped the other one below the elbow and began manipulating it back and forth. At the first touch, Caroline gave a little cry of pain.

"Steady now," urged the Earl.

She gritted her teeth together and did not cry out again.

Sweat began to bead on her forehead, and as the pain became worse her nails dug into Davenport's wrist, nearly drawing blood.

"Just a little bit more," muttered the doctor.

"Hurry, man, for God's sake," snapped Davenport.

With a last wrench the bone popped back into the socket. Caroline collapsed back against the pillow, her face as bleached as the surrounding sheets.

"Brave girl, well done." Davenport unconsciously brushed a damp tendril of hair from her brow as he spoke.

Caroline managed a weak smile. "Not missish . . . didn't throw a fit of vapors . . ."

"No, indeed."

She began to speak again then was suddenly, violently, sick.

The Earl stared down in dismay at his ruined shirt and breeches. An oath escaped his lips.

The doctor cleared his throat. "I shall call for Mrs. Collins. I'm sure she will be able to take care of . . . tidying up." He placed a small vial on the table. "Here is more laudanum for the pain she will undoubtedly feel when she wakes. Mrs. Collins knows the dose." He snapped his bag shut and regarded the Earl with what Davenport could swear was a glint of amusement. "Shall you be able to manage?"

Davenport muttered something unintelligible under his breath.

"I shall call again tomorrow morning. Have a pleasant day, my lord."

Davenport sighed as he kicked off his boots and stretched his stockinged toes towards the sputtering fire. Good Lord, it was more difficult than he imagined. His eyes strayed to the open ledger book on his desk. No matter how he juggled the columns, the debts were staggering and it would be some time before he could hope to make a dent in them. Perhaps Sykes was right. . . . His jaw tightened. Even though the family honor had meant nothing to his father or his brother, he was determined to do all in his power to see that it sank no further. Even without the promise to his mother, he would have done no less. But he had lived up to his word, he thought grimly, though she had no idea what it had cost him. The price to restore Highwood would be paltry in comparison. With a sigh, he took up the poker and raked out the dying embers.

Upstairs, as he made his way to his bedchamber, he was startled by a noise coming from the room of his mysterious stranger. He paused for a moment, then pushed open the heavy oak door at the sound of another cry. She was having a nightmare. Her shoulders writhed beneath the coverlet as if she were trying to struggle free from some imagined bonds.

"No!" she gasped weakly. "No!"

Davenport put down his candle and took her hand. It immediately tightened around his, surprising him with the strength in the slender fingers.

"Tell him . . ." she muttered.

He bent his ear close to her lips. "Tell him what?" he asked softly.

Her breathing was rapid, ragged. "Don't worry—I . . ." Her voice was barely there. "I can take care of myself." Then she fell silent.

The Earl held her hand until he felt the tension ebb out of her grip and her breathing settle back into a regular pattern. Tucking her hand carefully back under the covers, he left for his own room, to face his own demons.

Chapter Three

The doctor left off probing at Caroline's shoulder and stepped back with a satisfied look on his face. "You are recovering from your injuries remarkably well, miss. Another day of bed rest and you may begin to get up and move around. Of course, your arm will take longer to mend. I imagine it will ache like the devil for some time." He paused and gave her an appraising look. "I must tell you, well, I've never seen a female show the fortitude of . . ."

"Of a man?" she suggested, a slight smile stealing over her lips. "I'm not sure whether to take that as a compliment or an insult."

"Oh, for you miss, quite the first, I assure you." He rose to leave. "I shall call again in a few days. In the meantime, Mrs. Collins will see to it that you build your strength and his lordship . . ." He trailed off.

Caroline found herself wondering just what his lordship would see to.

"Good day to you, miss. And good luck."

Caroline nodded absently. Well, she would no doubt find out the Earl's intentions soon enough.

True to the doctor's expectations, Mrs. Collins did arrive a short while later with a tray of steaming porridge and pot of tea. Caroline submitted to the housekeeper's ministrations even though she felt capable of feeding herself, for it gave her the opportunity to learn more about her surroundings between bites.

"Why, Hemphill is the closest village. Ye ain't from around there, then?"

Caroline took a long swallow of tea, then quickly changed the subject. "Please thank her ladyship for the loan of a nightdress. I'm most grateful for the kindness."

"Can't," replied Mrs.Collins. "Thank her, that is. She ain't around anymore."

Caroline wondered what the housekeeper meant by that indelicate phrasing. Was he a widower? That would account for his rather gruff demeanor, especially if he was only recently bereaved. Or perhaps his was like many marriages of the *ton*, one of convenience rather than any mutual affection, and his wife spent her time in London or—

"I expect there are some other things in the attic that will fit," continued the other woman. Her expression indicated what she thought of Caroline's plan to take a needle to her own ragged garments. "I'll have a look up there as soon as you are finished with your meal."

"But perhaps, well, perhaps his lordship would be upset?"

Mrs. Collins shrugged. "Whyever should he care?"

Caroline took a few swallows of the hot, fragrant tea. She wasn't sure how to answer, but she found herself growing more and more curious about the Earl. "Does his lordship spend most of his days out overseeing his estate?"

The housekeeper gave a snort. "If that's what ye still call this place. But I give him credit. There's not many gentlemen would strip off their shirts and work along with his tenants." She must have noticed the look of disbelief on Caroline's face. "Aye," she nodded. "Shoulder to shoulder with 'em in the fields, that's a fact."

"How strange."

"Place is mortgaged to the hilt, so they say. Who knows how long afore the creditors foreclose. If there was other decent work to be had, I'd leave in a trice." Mrs. Collins,

naturally garrulous, was taking full advantage of a fresh—
and captive—audience. "Not that it's all that bad here,
mind you. Most of the house is closed up, under Holland
covers, so the work is manageable for me. Only other help
is Owens and the cook, but his lordship don't seem to need
much. . . ."

The butler stuck his head into the room. "Mrs. Collins,
Cook is threatening to give notice unless credit is extended
at the butcher's. Says she won't waste her talents baking
bread and slicing cheese."

The housekeeper muttered something under her breath
regarding the cook's culinary talents. "Well, I better go see
to her. It looks as if yer finished here anyway, miss." She
gathered up the dishes. "I shall visit the attic and see what I
can find after I've dealt with the kitchen."

Mrs. Collins was as good as her word. She reappeared
later with an armful of things, all in muted, if not somber,
colors. The Earl's late wife was apparently not of a lively
nature. It was all of good quality, however, and Caroline
was grateful though still hesitant about the propriety of
accepting her ladyship's clothing without the Earl's approval.

"You are sure it won't upset his lordship?" she asked
while eyeing the dark merino day dress that the housekeeper had draped over the foot of the bed. "I mean . . ."

But the other woman had already bustled from the room
in response to a shriek coming from downstairs.

Caroline slowly stood up. She still felt slightly woozy
and dreadfully sore from all her knocks and bruises. But
she forced herself to dress. She had lain about entirely too
long. Now that she had recovered her senses, at least, she
must resolve on a course of action.

As she fumbled with the buttons of the gown, she
thought about her current situation. Her reticule was lying
somewhere in the shattered remains of the carriage so she

hadn't a penny to her name. Name. Now that was a problem. Not only was she set on not revealing her own, but she had no idea whose house she was in. He had told her his name, that she remembered vaguely. But she couldn't for the life of her recall what it was. Darrencott . . . Dovepot—it was no use. She must remember to ask Mrs. Collins at the first opportunity to avoid making a cake of herself. However, she did know one thing. He was a gentleman, and as such, he would be expected to offer her assistance without asking awkward questions.

There wasn't a soul around when she made her way downstairs. No doubt Mrs. Collins and Owens were busy putting fires out in the kitchen. Curious, Caroline decided to look around on her own. Immediately to her right was the drawing room. It was done in shades of rose and emerald that had faded into lifeless shadows of their former hues. The carpets were threadbare and the mahogony sideboard, though recently waxed, showed its nicks and dents with little grace. Even the cushions on the sofas and wing chairs had a deflated look, as if depressed by all they had witnessed.

Her eyes strayed to the carved fireplace. Above the mantel hung a large painting of an extremely elegant gentleman. The style of dress—the ornately tied cravat, the multicolored figured silk waistcoat, perfectly tailored swallow-tail coat and snug-fitting pantaloons—was a total contrast, but the chiseled features were unmistakable, though there was a hardness to the mouth and eyes she hadn't noticed. . . .

"A fine painting, is it not?"

Caroline whirled around with a start.

"Forgive me for startling you," said Davenport as he took a step into the room. His gaze also moved to the portrait and his mouth quirked slightly. "The likeness is quite striking, don't you think?"

Caroline regarded his work-stained shirt, his shabby coat and buckskins, then turned back to stare at the gilt-framed canvas for what seemed like ages.

"No," she finally answered. "I do not."

His lips curled in a sardonic smile. "Ah, the difference in dress . . ."

"It isn't that." She knew that the prudent course of action would have been to remain silent but something goaded her to go on. "There is a certain cruelty about the mouth and the eyes—I wonder that you should tolerate it to be shown at all. It does you no credit."

Davenport's face betrayed a flicker of surprise. He stared thoughtfully at the portrait before returning his attention to Caroline. "Do you think it wise to be up and moving about so soon?" he inquired, abruptly changing the subject.

"I am unused to lying abed," she replied, then had the grace to color as she realized how boorish her actions, as well as her words, must appear. "Forgive me for wandering around your house uninvited."

Davenport shrugged. "You may do as you please—we do not stand on manners here at Highwood." Again, the hint of a sardonic smile.

"Highwood?" she repeated softly. "I do not recognize . . ." Her brow furrowed slightly as she pondered her dilemma. Finally she decided to settle it herself. "I find I must ask for your forgiveness again, my lord. I seem to recall that you introduced yourself earlier, but I—I cannot remember your name."

The smile deepened into real humor. "I believe you had other things to occupy your mind. I trust your arm is feeling better?" He inclined in a slight bow. "I am Davenport."

Caroline stepped back with an involuntarily gasp. "The *Earl* of Davenport?" she said, in barely more than a whisper.

"Ah, how heartening to be recognized." His tone was almost amused, but a flicker of some deeper emotion flashed in his smoky eyes.

She could only stare at him in disbelief. What wretched luck! Of all the places she could have stumbled into, she had to end up on the doorstep of one of the most dissolute rakehells in England. Oh yes, she knew of Davenport. His scandalous behavior was whispered about among the *ton*, and Caroline was well aware of the gossip, even though unmarried young ladies were not supposed to have their ears sullied with such shocking stories. Having a cousin who did not treat her as if she was a delicate—and witless—little creature had its uses.

He was regarding her as well, an inscrutable expression on his face. Finally, he shifted his weight from one booted foot to the other and broke the silence. "You needn't collapse in a paroxysm of terror. I prefer to choose my own victims. You, it appears, are already spoken for."

As Caroline went pale with anger, he walked past her to the sideboard and poured himself a brandy. "As I said, we do not stand on ceremony here. It has been a long day and I am devilishly thirsty. Would you care to join me?"

She shook her head.

"No, I didn't think so." The lips were curled once again in a faint smile. Furious as she was at his cutting words, Caroline could not help but notice there seemed to be a twinkle in his eye rather than the reptilian coldness portrayed on the canvas. "You are looking a trifle pale. Perhaps you should sit down before you fall into a faint."

"I have never had a fit of vapors in my life," she snapped. "I cannot imagine a more absurd reaction to troubling news. That is just the sort of time you need your wits about you."

He threw back his head and laughed. It was a very pleasant sound. "You have a good deal of spirit, Miss. . . ." He looked at her expectantly.

She clamped her teeth shut.

"Hmmm." He cocked his head to one side. "I shall have to call you something." He looked her up and down, his eyes lingering on the arm that had been injured. "Miss Socket." His gaze traveled up to her face. "Miss Gash. Miss Hurt."

Her lips began to twitch.

"Ah, I have it!" He rubbed at his nose. "Miss Boxer!"

At that she couldn't repress a smile of her own. "Are you always so absurd, sir?"

"No. Usually it takes until the third or fourth brandy."

Caroline's face instantly turned stony. How had she let herself be drawn into bantering with such a man? She had come downstairs with a purpose and she had let herself be distracted.

"I must leave here immediately," she announced.

Davenport removed his dusty coat and sank into a faded wing chair. He wore no cravat and his shirt was open at the neck, revealing a hint of dark curls under the rumpled linen. "I am relieved to hear it, Miss Boxer. I have more than enough of my own problems to manage without having to deal with some gothic female. Good luck to you—you appear to need it."

Caroline stood with her mouth agape. That was not exactly the response she had expected. Surely even a gentleman as jaded as the Earl would offer her the use of his carriage!

She began again. "Sir, what I meant was, I should be obliged if you would have your carriage brought around to take me on to . . . to my destination as soon as possible."

His bark of laughter was short and humorless. "Forgive my rudeness, Miss Boxer, but have you had a closer look around? There *is* no carriage. And the only animal in the stables besides my stallion is a rather ordinary hack."

She swallowed. "Perhaps a carriage may be hired?"

He crossed his legs nonchalantly. "Have you any money?"

She shook her head.

"Well, neither have I, at least none to spare for a private conveyance for you. I'm barely scraping by as it is. Perhaps you have relatives you can send word to?"

Caroline bit her lip. She was saved from having to reply by the entrance of Mrs. Collins, carrying a tray with a few slices of cold ham, a chunk of bread and some Stilton cheese. "I have your supper here, my lord, as you asked." She hadn't noticed Caroline standing to the side. She set it down on a side table and ran her hands over the front of her apron. "The candle-maker's son just brought out a package for me and said someone—a gentleman of Quality by the sounds of it—is inquiring in the village whether any strange young ladies have passed through recently—" She was interrupted by a horrified gasp.

Caroline had turned deathly pale. Her hand flew to her throat. For a moment, she was mortally afraid that she would have to eat her words concerning a certain habit.

"Don't you worry none, miss," said Mrs. Collins quickly. "I know when to keep mum. I seen what he done to you."

How had he found her so quickly?

Davenport regarded her intently. "You are safe here," he said quietly. Then he rubbed at his temples and muttered something that sounded suspiciously like an oath. "Perhaps in the morning we can figure a way out of this coil."

Caroline fought to compose her voice. "If you will excuse me, I'm feeling rather fatigued. I think I shall return to my room."

Caroline closed the door to her chamber. Much too agitated to lie down, she began to pace the narrow confines. Was her nemesis possessed of preternatural powers? She had thought herself safe from any pursuit for at least a few more days. A shudder passed through her and she had to fight down a rising wave of panic. Then her eyes fell on the ragged dress draped over the back of the chair. She would not—could not—let those papers fall into the wrong hands. That thought helped steady her nerves. What was it Lucien always told her when she was younger and hesitated at following him up to the highest boughs of the tree or setting her horse at a difficult jump?

That the only enemy was fear itself.

She cajoled herself to think. What would Lucien do? Most certainly he would not cower like a frightened mouse waiting for the snake to strike. He would take action. And so would she.

Her pacing became less frantic as she fell deep in thought. First of all, it appeared she could expect no help from the infamous Earl of Davenport. But she supposed she should still count herself fortunate in some respects. Not having a feather to fly with, if he could be believed, had appeared to have curbed some of his more flagrant excesses. There was no sign that any wild debauches were going to occur while she was under his roof, so her person seemed safe enough from him, at least for the time being.

However, his claim to poverty did appear to have the ring of truth. Even the most cursory look around had revealed a household shackled by the strictest economy—the shabby furnishings, the lack of servants, the simple supper taken off a tray. Her brow furrowed. The notion of the Earl's pockets being to let certainly jibed with her understanding of his character. No doubt he was rusticating in the country to hide from his most pressing creditors. But the thought of the dissolute Earl actually stooping to manual labor was nearly as implausible as her own predicament. Caroline shook her head slightly and decided it was best to put the man out of her thoughts. After all, his predicament was not her concern, just as hers was obviously of no interest to him. It was solely up to her to come up with a plan.

The hem of her dress caught on the foot of the bed and she yanked at it impatiently. As her hands smoothed the folds of the borrowed garment she couldn't help but mutter an unladylike oath. Men had such fewer constraints on them in dress, in behavior, in freedom to move about. . . .

She stopped dead in her tracks.

The merino wool was still between her fingers and she played with the cloth as her mind raced. It was not a bad idea at all. It certainly wouldn't be the first time she had ever tried it. There was the time that Lucien had taken her to see Cribbs step into the ring with the challenger from the north. . . . She could pull it off, she was sure she could.

Her mind made up, she forced herself to lie down. She would need her strength, and besides, she could not put her plan into action until well after midnight. There were no servants to worry about. She could only hope that the Earl had not abandoned all of his profligate tendencies and would indulge freely in the bottle, as wastrels were wont to do. Then she remembered the distinctive aroma that had enveloped his person on both the mornings she had encountered him. Her lips curled in a slight smile. Yes, there was no doubt he would be in a drunken stupor by that hour.

Some hours later, she quietly crept into the dark hallway. She dared not light her candle just yet, but a pale wash of moonlight from a window near her door gave just enough illumination for her to find her way without incident. She had an idea of where she was going, for though she had dozed off and on throughout the afternoon, she couldn't help but hear the sturdy tramp of Mrs. Collins climbing up and down the stairs. Slowly she moved along the threadbare carpet. Her throat tightened at the thought that she might inadvertently stumble into the Earl's bedchamber, but she forced herself to relax. It was highly unlikely he would notice, even if she did. By this time he no doubt had his hand well entwined around the smooth form of a bottle—or something equally as warming. In either case, his attention would be fully occupied.

She paused before a closed door. It seemed the likely one. Slowly she turned the handle and pushed it open a few inches. A sigh of relief escaped her lips. Wooden stairs. She slipped inside and pulled the door shut. It was even colder in the attic than in the rest of the house and she shivered slightly in the pitch dark as she fumbled to light her candle. A sudden draft reminded her to look for a warm jacket as well the other things she had in mind. The flame lit, she hurried up into the cavernous darkness, her stockinged feet making no more noise than a scurrying mouse on the dusty treads.

A short time later, Caroline emerged from the doorway, her arms laden with an assortment of things. She crept back to her room and laid out the items she had selected on the bed. As she had suspected, very little had been thrown out over the generations. She had exactly what she needed.

Stepping back from the mirror, she adjusted the over-sized woolen cap so that it fell even lower over her eyes. The effect was perfect. She tucked in the tails of the rough cotton, marveling again at how much freer she felt already, unencumbered by yards of material falling around her legs. The leather boots were a little too large, but it was of no matter. At least the thick wool socks kept her toes feeling warm. Shrugging into the heavy jacket, she was not unhappy that it, too, was a trifle big. It helped camouflage certain parts of her anatomy that were best left unseen. She took it off again and carefully felt around in its lining. It would do. She fetched her old gown and the sewing things Mrs. Collins had left for her. The transfer of the oiled packet holding the papers took only a few minutes—she hadn't been bamming the housekeeper, she was rather skilled with a needle. As she put the garment back on, she looked out the window. A hint of light was just beginning to edge its way to the horizon. Even if there was a groom, he would not be up for another hour or two.

It was time to go.

Davenport splashed cold water onto his face from the pitcher on his dresser. He had slept fitfully and felt the dragging lethargy of one not fully rested. Still, it was futile to stay in bed. His mind was too preoccupied with his mounting problems, not least of which was the damned young lady peacefully asleep down the hall.

He didn't doubt for a moment that lady she was, and not some farmer's wife or daughter. Her hands were smooth and soft, showing no signs of labor. Her speech was too cultured, not to speak of her knowledge of Society—after all, she knew exactly who *he* was.

The question was, who was *she?*

Her clothes certainly didn't indicate she came from a highborn family. But then again, he thought with an ironic smile, dress didn't always indicate pedigree. It could also be a disguise. If she were fleeing someone, she would no doubt seek to obscure her background. His lips compressed in a tight line. He didn't have the time or energy for such gothic melodramas. He meant to have the truth out of her this morning and that was that. Then he could get her out of his life.

But could he truly hand her over to someone who had darkened her face in such a brutish manner?

He swore under his breath as he dried his stubbled chin. A grimace came over his features as the towel scraped over the thin line of scar tissue. His fingers came up to rub absently along the ridge of his cheekbone. Why did it always ache like the devil when he was tired and agitated? Lord, he needed some fresh air. A gallop on Nero would do him good, despite the early hour. Surely he would think of something by the time he returned.

It was barely light as he made his way towards the stable. He was so preoccupied with his thoughts that he almost missed the flicker of movement in the interior shadows. He stopped short, his grip instinctively tightening around his crop. His dark brows came together—something was amiss. Then it struck him. The doors shouldn't be ajar like that. Higgins wouldn't be up and about his duties for a good while yet—nothing short of Gabriel sounding the final awakening would induce the old man out of his bed until it was absolutely necessary.

Davenport started forward again, slowly, quietly, every muscle tensed. At that moment, a lad of no more than fifteen or sixteen years emerged from the murky depths of the building, leading a fully saddled Nero. The Earl's jaw dropped in disbelief.

The scamp was stealing his horse!

"You there! Stand where you are!" he bellowed as he broke into a run.

The lad's head came up with a start. He appeared frozen for a second but then moved with astonishing quickness. Thrusting a boot into the shortened stirrups, he vaulted into the saddle and jammed his heels into the stallion's flanks. Nero tossed his head wildly and shied to one side, but the boy handled the reins with skill. His heels came down again, urging the animal forward. Davenport's outstretched hand missed the bridle by inches.

"Damnation!" he roared as he skittered to a stop and watched them gallop out across the field.

But luck was with him. As the horse came to the edge of the woods, the boy chose the cart path to the right. The Earl still had a chance to catch them. He turned and ran into the stable. Cursing roundly as he barked his shins more than once in the darkness, he found the other saddle and bridle and hurried to the stall of his other horse. The animal had no chance of catching a prime goer like Nero, but he didn't have to. Davenport finished tightening the girth and mounted, an ominous expression on his face. He set his own mount off at a good clip. Unless the lad had an intimate knowledge of the area, he would stick to the beaten path.

Well, if he did, he was going to run into a little surprise.

Davenport guided his mount through an adjoining field. They cleared a tumbled stone wall and skirted the edge of a newly planted field of wheat. In the middle of a large copse of beeches, the earl guided his horse onto a narrow trail, barely wide enough to pass through without the branches slapping at his boots and breeches. They emerged at right angles to a wider path, whose ruts and ridges gave evidence of frequent cart travel. Davenport smiled in grim satisfaction and reined his horse to a halt. It appeared they were in time. In the distance, he could hear the muffled rhythm of pounding hooves.

A dark shape rounded the corner. The Earl could just make out the lad's head bent low over Nero's neck, still urging the big stallion to give his best effort. And no doubt Nero was in clover. There was nothing he liked better than to be allowed to race neck and leather through the country-side.

Traitor, thought Davenport sourly as he readied his own horse to match strides with him.

The thief had the benefit of speed and stamina while Davenport had the element of surprise. The Earl liked his chances.

As his stallion approached, Davenport charged from the cover of the trees. He drew alongside and reached for the reins. Nero shied violently to the right. Knowing his stallion's habits, Davenport was ready for it. The lad was not. As the Earl's hand instinctively followed the movement of

the horse's head, the sudden change of stride pitched the
young rider forward. He lost his stirrups and slipped sideways from the saddle. Both of his hands clung to the edges
of the leather while his feet hung precariously close to the
flailing hooves. The Earl managed to grab the reins and
fought to bring the spooked stallion under control. Suddenly, with a sharp yelp of pain, the lad's grip gave out with
one of his hands. In another moment he would be trampled.

Serves him right, thought Davenport to himself. His own
neck was at risk too, trying to manage two wildly galloping
animals. But with a silent curse he let go of Nero and
reached down to grab the lad by the collar of his jacket.

"Let go!" he shouted, as he reined in on his own mount.

The youngster needed no encouragement. His strength
was gone and the last of his fingers slipped from the saddle.
Davenport's mount was too winded to offer any resistance
to the pressure on the reins. The animal slowed to a trot,
then stopped dead in its tracks, sides heaving and sweat
lathering its flanks. The Earl held the young thief by the
scruff of his jacket, as if he were disposing of a weasel
from a dovecote. It took great restraint not to wring the
lad's neck as he would that of an offending predator. Instead he satisfied himself by dropping the lad none too gently onto the rutted ground.

"You damn young fool," cursed the Earl as he dismounted. "I should take my crop to you. Don't you know
you could be trans—"

It was then that he noticed that the lad's hat had fallen
off. There was a mass of hair, honey-colored hair, spilling
over the pale face. His eyes traveled lower, to where a pair
of slender—and very shapely—thighs were revealed by a
pair of tight buckskin breeches. With a start he realized
they were *his* breeches, from when he was a boy.

He closed his eyes and groaned.

Caroline lay in the dirt, too stunned to move. The pain in

her shoulder was so intense that she could taste bile in the back of her throat.

"You!" roared Davenport. His face had lost the look of blank surprise and was now clouded with anger. "You nearly got both of us killed! What the bloody hell were you thinking, trying to ride a blooded stallion?"

She struggled to a sitting position, clutching at her arm. The oversized jacket had slipped on her shoulder, making her look even smaller and more vulnerable. Her face was pinched and streaked with mud while her lips were pressed tightly together, trying to suppress the slight quiver at their corners. Yet when she looked up at him her eyes held only a spirited determination. "I ride as well as any man—it was you who caused the problem by charging out of the bushes like a . . . a highwayman," she managed to retort.

His jaw dropped in astonishment. "A bloody highway-man," he sputtered. "You impudent chit. You were stealing my horse!"

"I wasn't exactly stealing him. I was going to give him back." She brushed away the loose curls that had fallen to obscure half of her face. It was obvious he was furious. She knew the prudent course of action was to remain silent, to allow his anger to simmer down from its initial boil. But for some reason she couldn't stop herself from going on, more because defiance helped keep her own half frightened spirits up than to intentionally goad him on.

"You know, you should give him his head more often—a top-of-the-trees horse like that needs a good run to keep him up to snuff."

Davenport wasn't sure he had heard correctly. "What?" he asked in an ominously low voice.

"I said, I hope you know how to handle him properly."

His eyes were as dark as smoldering embers. "You call that handling him properly, flying neck and leather out of control? It's a wonder he didn't throw you sooner."

"I was not out of control! I'll have you know I have been riding blooded stallions since I was six and can handle a mount as well—or better—than most men."

He couldn't quite believe he was standing here brangling with her. His eyes went down to her breeches and boots. "So you like something spirited between your legs?" he snapped.

Caroline's eyes followed his. She had worn breeches around Lucien and her father's grooms for ages, but suddenly her legs looked, well, nearly naked. Color flooded her face and unconsciously she curled up like a hedgehog. The movement sent a jolt of pain shooting through her shoulder, causing her to bite her lip nearly hard enough to draw blood.

He looked as if to say something, then walked over to where she lay. "Are you all right?" he asked curtly.

She nodded, not trusting herself to speak. She was determined not to disgrace herself by crying out or casting up her accounts for the second time in front of the Earl. She would take whatever punishment he chose to mete out like . . . a man. Rumor had it the man possessed a devil of a temper. What would he—

He reached down and lifted her to her feet. When her legs buckled slightly, his arm came around her waist. "Come. Sit down over here."

He guided her to a fallen tree by the side of the path and settled her on its broad trunk. Neither of them spoke for several moments. Caroline took a few deep breaths and the pain and dizziness subsided.

"Better?"

She nodded again.

Davenport turned to stare down at the dirt farm track. His jaw clenched and the sparks in his eyes betrayed the war that was raging within. Finally, he cleared his throat. "I apologize," he muttered through gritted teeth. "That was an unpardonable remark." He shook his head in disbelief. "The chit steals my horse and here I am apologizing," he continued to himself. His fingers moved absently to his cheekbone and began to massage the thin white line running across it.

Caroline slanted him a sideways glance. "I'm sorry as well. I know I . . . provoked you. Truly, I did not wish to steal your horse, but you wouldn't help me. I had no choice. You don't understand—I have to get away from here." Her hands tightened in her lap. "Right now."

Davenport let out a exasperated sigh. "We will discuss this in a more suitable place. Will you be all right for a moment while I fetch Nero?"

A strangled sound came from Caroline. He thought for a moment that she was finally succumbing to girlish hysterics then realized she was trying not to laugh.

"Oh, tell me a man of your reputation didn't really name his horse Nero," she managed to say in answer to his quizzical look.

His lips twitched at the corners. "One must have a sense of humor to survive in this world."

Chapter Four

Caroline wasn't sure the Earl's study was exactly the spot she would have chosen for their confrontation. He looked even more forbidding seated behind the massive oak desk, hands steepled before him on the tooled blotter, stormy blue eyes crashing into her like waves against the strand. It was uncomfortably familiar, having faced her father under similar situations on countless occasions. Besides, there was the little matter of . . .

"And now, Miss—" There was an emphatic pause, which he drew out like a duelist unsheathing a rapier. His voice, though low, was equally sharp. "Kindly put an end to the theatrics. If you wish to continue enacting a Cheltenham tragedy, join Mrs. Siddons on the boards—I will not tolerate it any longer under my roof. I mean to know who you are, and I mean to know it *now*."

It was only in the last sentence that the volume rose drastically. But if the desired effect was to reduce the young lady seated before him to flinging herself at his feet in contrition and immediately confessing her identity, he had sadly miscalculated his own oratorical skills.

Caroline's head hunched down towards her shoulders and her face took on an expression that one of the brasher young grooms at Roxbury had characterized as "mulish."

There was nothing but silence.

Davenport's gaze continued to wash over her, the blue of his eyes darkening to a scudding gray. His fingers began drumming on the scarred wood. When it became evident that words were not forthcoming, he rose and slowly walked to stand beside her chair. Caroline was not lacking in stature herself, but from where she was seated, the Earl seemed to tower over her, his broad shoulders and powerful torso only reinforcing the appearance of holding the upper hand. She imagined that was the intention.

The nerve of the man, to think he could bully her with his ultimatums!

She resolutely refused to look up at him. Instead, she locked her gaze on the first item on his desk that caught her eye. As she focused in on it, she found that for the second time that morning she had to strangle the urge to laugh. It was a book. On the breeding of sheep.

"Well?" It came out as a baritone rumble.

"It is *you*, sir, who may stop the histrionics. They do not intimidate me. I will not tell you my name. It is of no concern to you in any case."

Outrage flared in Davenport's breast. "When I am forced to drag some half-dead chit out of the mud, have her nursed back to health at an expense I can ill afford, only to have her steal my property . . ."

Caroline had the grace to color.

". . . then it damn well is my concern. I mean to have your name, make no mistake about it." His eyes narrowed. "Perhaps I should just haul you into the village—it seems there I should learn who you are soon enough."

Caroline shot up from her chair. "The only mistake I have made is landing on the doorstep of a profligate wastrel who has squandered his last farthing on drinking and gaming and . . . and other pursuits, no doubt, instead of taking care of his responsibilities, like a true gentleman. Why, it seems you are insensible to even the most basic decencies of your class, like helping a lady in distress, you—you odious man!"

Davenport's patience, already dangerously frayed, snapped. For weeks he had borne the shrill demands of countless creditors, the suspicious looks of his tenants, the whispered innuendos of his neighbors. More nights than he cared to remember he had struggled with the ledger books, fighting against despair to come up with a way to restore his estate and family name to respectability. She spoke of common decencies—what of Helen? To be so cavalierly accused by a chit barely out of the schoolroom, with no acquaintance of him except through rumor, was too much to bear, especially when she owed him her very life. How dare she speak to him like that?

His hand came up in the air.

Caroline flinched, more at the look in his eyes than from the threat of physical violence. They were flooded with anger, but there was something more. In their depths was an expression of intense pain.

Davenport caught himself. Is that how it began? he wondered. A simple loss of temper that suddenly moves from thought to deed? The bruises on the face before him, though lightened, were still very much in evidence, ugly, raw reminders of somebody else's anger. He thought of Helen's face, how similar the damage looked. Except her eyes did not spark with spirit anymore as this young lady's did. How many times did it take to beat the will out of another person? His jaw clenched. And why would someone filled with life and humor and dreams allow it?

The thought of how easy it would have been to cross the line made him nearly ill. Was he really not so very different from Charles after all? He had never been so utterly ashamed of himself. His hand fell to his side and he moved slowly around to slump into his chair. Running his hand through his hair, he turned to stare, unseeing, into the cold black coals of the unlit fireplace.

"What would you have me do?" he asked in a voice barely above a whisper. "I have a small sum . . ."

Caroline cleared her throat. "Ahh . . . actually, sir, you do not." She took the leather purse she had removed from the Earl's desk earlier that morning out of the pocket of her jacket and laid it in front of him.

For a brief moment, Davenport wondered if he was beginning to lose his sanity. He stared at it, speechless. Then he threw back his head and began to laugh.

It was a pleasant sound, a rich mellifluous baritone that rang true to the ear. She also noticed that he really had the most expressive eyes. Just then they had softened, the color lightened by humor to a hue as airy as the sky. Minutes before, when he had been so angry, they had been as impervious as slate. There was a raw complexity too, but never the cold, calculated cruelty depicted by the painting in the next room.

The sound of his laughter trailed off and his face took on an expression of bemused resignation. "Seeing as I am at my wit's end, perhaps you have some idea as to how to proceed." His glance traveled over her breeches and boots once more. "You seem to have no lack of imagination."

Caroline sat down abruptly. "As a matter of fact, I do have a proposal."

His mouth twitched at the corners. "I rather thought you might. Well, let's have it."

She squared her shoulders. "You are obviously in dire need of funds. I am in dire need of reaching a certain destination without further delay. So I propose a partnership of sorts. If you will help me get there, I will pay you very well."

"And just where are you going?"

Caroline hesitated for a moment. There was little sense on prevaricating on that point. "London."

"How much?"

"A thousand pounds."

Davenport gave a bark of laughter. "Good Lord, are you truly intent on making a monkey of me this morning? Or have you received another knock on the head, one that has caused you take leave of your senses?" He shook his head. "A thousand pounds, indeed."

"It is no joke, sir," said Caroline indignantly. "I promise you, when we reach London you shall have it."

He merely chuckled. "Yes, I shall eat gooseberry tarts perched atop Parliament, too."

"You doubt my word?"

He stopped laughing.

"Do you?" she persisted. "No doubt you would not think of insulting a man's honor by refusing to accept his word."

The Earl's brows came together thoughtfully. "Hmmm." Once again his fingers began drumming on the desk as he mulled over her words. The fact of the matter was, he needed to pay a visit to his man of affairs in Town at some point soon. And even though the odds were her offer was merely a desperate ploy, in the event that her family would be grateful, he could sorely use a thousand pounds. But there was something else as well, something oddly touching about her pluck . . .

"Let me make sure I understand you," he said very slowly. "You wish to *hire* me to escort you to London, for which service I will receive one thousand pounds?"

"That is correct, my lord."

"Very well, we have a deal, Miss . . ."

"My name is Caroline."

"Truly?"

She nodded. "Yes, but other than that I shall not say."

His lips pursed but he did not argue. He merely leaned back in his chair and leveled on her a piercing gaze. "Now that my role is little more than a hired lackey, have you given any thought as to how we may travel to London? I take it you have inspected the stables well enough to know I wasn't telling you a hum when I said there is no carriage." He picked up the meager purse and let it drop again. "I doubt there is enough for two fares on the mail coach, even if we take outside passage."

"But you have two horses. And they are already saddled."

"You have no proper riding clothes and—you can't mean . . ."

"That's exactly what I mean. It is the simplest and quickest means. I shall be your groom. Trust me, I'm quite good at pulling it off. Luc—a male cousin has on occasion taken me to mills and a tavern with no one the wiser."

He closed his eyes. "He should be birched." There was a slight pause. "You are serious, aren't you?"

"Have you another idea?" she challenged. When he didn't answer, her mouth set in a line of grim satisfaction. "Besides," she added, "no one will be looking for two men traveling east. Come, let's not waste any more time."

Davenport pushed back from his desk. "Do you mind if I have my damn breakfast first?" he snapped irritably. "Then I intend to pack a valise. And shave." His eyes strayed once again to her garb. "I suppose we ought to take another look in the attic as well. You'll need . . . some other things if we are to carry on with this harebrained idea." He shook his head slowly. "*I* should be birched, though I fear I shall face far worse before this is all over."

She smiled sweetly. "Of course, please see to anything you feel is necessary, my lord. As long as we are ready to leave in, say forty-five minutes?"

He stalked from the room, muttering darkly under his breath.

Caroline took a sip of tea and nibbled at a piece of toast from the tray that the Earl had sent in to her. It seemed Fortune had looked kindly on her at last. Despite her boast to the Earl, the thought of traveling alone, disguised as a man, having to brave the ostlers, the common rooms, the long stretches of deserted roads was a daunting, if not terrifying thought. It would be nice to have a companion, however ill-tempered.

Good Lord, he had been angry, angry enough to strike out at her. She would not have blamed him if he had, for she knew she had goaded him unmercifully with her quick tongue. Her lips compressed ruefully as she recalled how many times both her father and Lucien had warned her that a lady must learn to curb her emotions or risk placing herself beyond the pale. But the Earl had held back. Some emotion she couldn't decipher had flickered through his eyes at the last minute, holding him back. It was as if he was . . . ashamed of his actions.

That puzzled her. A rakehell wasn't supposed to have any emotions, at least not any decent one. Or perhaps she had misunderstood Lucien's whispered explanations on the subject—it was so annoying having to depend on someone else's experiences for information. Regardless, it appeared the Earl of Davenport was not entirely without feeling. He could very well have let her slip to her death under the pounding hooves and not a soul would have blamed him. And then, his arm around her waist had been nearly gentle as he had helped her recover. It was all so very confusing. Even now, though he had stalked from the room in an ill temper, he had been thoughtful enough to send breakfast in to her.

She let her breath out in a sigh. No doubt it was best not to dwell on it overly—especially those interesting eyes and pleasant laugh. All she should care about was whether he could bring her safely to Town, nothing else.

A sharp rap came on the library door. Davenport stuck

his head into the room, making a point of letting his gaze linger on the clock on the mantel.

"Are you ready? Or, like most females, do you mean forty-five minutes to indicate we won't be leaving until after noon?"

Caroline brushed the crumbs from her breeches as she stood up and shrugged into her coat. The Earl waited as she paused by the mirror to tuck her hair up under the wool cap, then turned on his heel, leaving her to follow in his wake. He ignored the incredulous looks from both Mrs. Collins and Owens as the two of them strode through the entrance hall. Caroline managed a brief smile, then shot forward to keep the heavy oak door from slamming on her nose.

Outside, Davenport flung a leather portmanteau over Nero's flanks, then tied another set of bags at the back of the other horse's saddle. As he turned, he noticed Caroline looking with longing at the stallion.

"Don't even think of it," he growled.

Caroline sighed and let him give her a leg up onto the smaller mount. "My lord," she ventured as she set her boots into the stirrups, "I have one other question—are you armed?"

His eyes narrowed. "Do not let that lively imagination of yours run away with you. Though you may relish the idea of pistols at dawn and other such nonsense, I do not. You may rest assured that our journey will pass without incident."

For the first time, Caroline felt a stab of guilt. Did she truly have a right to bring another person into danger? The papers at her ribs were an all too uncomfortable reminder that what lay ahead was no ordinary journey. It was for their country, she reminded herself. Surely even a dissolute rake would feel honor-bound to help, if he knew the truth.

The Earl swung himself into the saddle and, without a backwards look, spurred his horse into a canter.

An hour later, Caroline found herself wondering if the Earl was going to utter a word during their journey. He ignored her presence and kept up a rapid pace without so much as a glance as to whether she was still with him. She set her jaw and used all of her considerable skill to keep up. From her position behind him she noted that he rode with an effortless grace, handling the spirited stallion with a subtle command rather than engaging in a heavy-handed battle of wills. The animal moved with confidence, exuberance even, yet there was no doubt as to who was in control. Grudgingly she admitted that in this, at least, he was bang up to the mark.

As they reached a long stretch of flat road, Davenport slowed his horse to a walk. Caroline urged her own mount forward to ride abreast with him.

"You ride tolerably well," he said curtly, before she had a chance to say anything. "You may count yourself lucky."

The compliment she had intended to make died on her lips. "What do you mean?"

"If you hadn't been able to keep up, I would have ended this harebrained scheme an hour ago." He paused. "I still might," he added under his breath.

Caroline's voice became heated. "But we have an agreement!"

"Yes," he replied coolly, not taking his eyes from the road ahead. "But be that as it may, if it had been beyond your powers, I'd not risk your neck—or mine. I've no intention of having to play nursemaid, no matter what the reward."

So he thought to manage her like his horse! Caroline reined in her temper, however, settling for what she considered a mild response.

"Satisfied?"

"For now."

She restrained the urge to deliver a swift kick to his shins.

After a strained silence, she tried another tack of questioning. "Are we to travel on back roads for the entire journey?"

"Do you wish to set the route as well?" he countered, a touch of sarcasm creeping into his tone.

She noticed that he avoided using her name, and in fact had ceased making even the slightest attempt at polite address—now it was not even "Miss." Really, the man was infuriating. But he was her only choice.

"As I am unfamiliar with this part of the country, it would be a useless endeavor on my part."

"Ah, something on which you are not the expert," he muttered acidly. "I hadn't thought it possible."

That struck her as unfair. "Are you always so deliberately rude to ladies?" she inquired through gritted teeth.

He finally turned to look at her. "Ladies?" His brows arched up as his eyes swept over her breeches, shabby coat and drooping cap. "I thought I was riding with my groom. As such, there is little need to be charming." With that, he spurred Nero into a trot.

Some time later, they made a brief stop beside a river to allow the horses to drink and take a short respite from the road. Davenport fished a packet of cold ham and a wedge of Stilton out of his bag along with half a loaf of bread and a bottle of cider. He laid everything out on the ground, and after helping himself to a good portion, went to stand with his back to her, looking out over the water as he ate.

His behavior was worse than boorish, decided Caroline as she picked at a few morsels. But then, what else should she expect from such a man? Why, he probably had no more sense of civility than his horse. If he was determined to be unspeakably rude throughout the entire trip, she would not give him the satisfaction of seeing that it piqued her. And she certainly wouldn't admit she wasn't up to matching his stamina, which was an admission he also seemed intent upon wresting from her. So though she dearly would have liked to linger and rest her aching limbs in the late morning sun, she hurriedly finished the last of her cheese and caught up the reins of her mount.

"Whenever you are ready," she called with a show of obvious impatience as she hoisted herself into the saddle.

Davenport threw the remains of his meal into the swirling currents and remounted without a word.

He was being unspeakably rude. He knew it, yet the knowledge only made him feel more disgruntled at his situation. It was his own fault, really, but that stark truth also did nothing to improve his humor. What the devil had caused him to agree to shepherd the young lady to London? The money? He wanted to tell himself it was that, but he knew the truth. Something in those sparkling eyes had revealed a touching vulnerability. And he, fool that he was, had been incapable of turning his back on it.

His hands tightened on the reins, causing the big stallion to shy to one side. With a silent curse, he patted the horse's neck in apology, then suddenly urged him into a full gallop, as if the effort could give vent to his anger. A string of oaths followed, all directed at himself. How had he been such a gudgeon once again, to let a helpless young lady use him to her advantage?

His mouth quirked involuntarily at the corners as he recalled the image of her pounding neck and leather out over the field on his stallion—perhaps "helpless" was not exactly the right word for this young lady. But then his jaw set as he wondered, not for the first time, why it seemed to be the cruel ones who attracted the opposite sex, like a moth to a flame. Helen's face came to mind, her porcelain skin suspiciously darkened, her eyes desperate, crying for help. He had forgiven her for turning to him after—but he had not forgiven himself.

It wouldn't ever happen again. He meant to care for nothing but himself now, nothing but his lands and restoring them and his name to respectability. This morning had been a regrettable lapse in judgment, but he had been tired and preoccupied with other problems. She had taken him by surprise. It was damned unfair of her to expect him to be her knight in shining armor.

Well, he wouldn't be. He would merely be the mercenary. Get her to her family, collect his blunt—if there truly was any to collect—and be gone, as quickly as possible. That was all she had hired him for. And that was all she would bloody well get.

It was damned unfair of him, she fumed as she coaxed her tired horse into a gallop. Why should he be so angry at her? She could hardly be accused of forcing him to agree to the deal. And he would be well paid for his effort. So what was causing him to act in such an unpleasant manner? Really, he was the most ill-tempered, ill-mannered gentleman she had ever encountered—but maybe that was because he was no gentleman.

It was strange, though, he did seem to have a streak of kindness, which he endeavored to keep buried, as if he were . . . embarrassed by it.

Her horse could no longer keep up. And she herself was so weary and aching that she could barely sit up in the saddle. She let the animal slow to a shuffling walk. If he wanted his money, he would damn well have to come back and get them. Otherwise . . . Her brows knitted together. He had what little funds they possessed. But she had a horse, and a disguise and a head start on whoever was . . .

It must have been the bright midday sun that made her

suddenly so very tired, for normally she would never, ever
have slipped from the saddle.

When Caroline's eyes fluttered open, she was lying by
the side of the dirt cart path, her head resting on one of her
saddlebags, the Earl's coat covering her from knee to chin.
She turned her head slightly, out of the glare. He was
stretched out beside her, propped up on his elbows, staring
off into the distance. His profile was to her, a pensive look
on his features. By the set of his jaw and the tiny lines of
strain etched at the corners of his eyes and mouth, it
seemed to her that he was waging some sort of internal battle. She studied his face carefully. It was a complex one, the
emotions not easily readable, as they were on someone less
guarded, like her cousin Lucien—Lord, she always knew
what he was thinking! But what truly puzzled her was that
even in catching him off guard, she still saw no hint of the
hardness, the cruelty so graphically depicted in the painting
above his mantel. It was not something so easily hidden.
Why, the artist had seen it as the essence of the man, yet
where was it? How could she miss such an obvious thing?

Davenport turned to her. "Awake, are you?"

She struggled to sit up. "I'm ready to . . ."

His hand caught her shoulder and kept her from rising.
"Rest a little longer. We needn't push on any harder today."

"I won't go back. . . ."

He smiled briefly. "No, I don't imagine you would. You
are a very determined young lady." He reached for the bottle of cider beside him and offered it to her.

"Groom," she corrected, gamely essaying a smile herself.
She sat up and took a long swallow. It was tepid and flat
but it tasted wonderful. "Thank you."

He nodded, suppressing another twitch of his lips.

Caroline turned her face to the sun and couldn't resist
taking off her cap and shaking out her hair. It cascaded over
her shoulders, glinting a pale amber in the bright light.

"Mmmm," she said softly, taking in the warmth. For a few minutes she just lay there. When she looked back up at him, he was regarding her with brows drawn together, mouth compressed in a tight line.

"Why are you so angry with me?" she asked.

His features quickly composed themselves into an impassive mask. "What makes you think I am angry with you?" Unconsciously, his hand came up to rub at the thin white line on his cheek.

"You do that quite often, you know. How did you get that scar?" she asked impulsively.

He stiffened.

"I'm sorry," she murmured. "I don't mean to upset you any further—it's just that if we are to be in each other's company until London, I thought it might be possible to have a conversation. If you would rather not . . ." She let the words trail off.

His breath came out in a sigh. "If you imagine it is an interesting story, you are quite mistaken. I was merely engaged in a fencing match with my brother. The button on his foil must have come off. The point caught my cheek before either of us noticed what had happened."

"Oh, he must have felt dreadful for cutting you so!"

Davenport gave a harsh laugh. "You think so?" Then he fell silent.

"Do the two of you not get along?"

"It hardly matters. He's dead."

She bit her lip. "I'm . . . sorry."

"I'm not." He got up abruptly to his feet and walked off towards where the horses were grazing.

She rose and followed him. He was checking the saddles and girths. "You needn't get up. Why don't you rest a little longer so I won't have to scrape you out of the mud yet again," he growled.

Caroline laid a hand on his forearm. "I'm truly sorry, my lord. I didn't mean to stir painful memories."

"Cut line—you have no idea what I am feeling," he snapped, brushing her hand away. He stopped short at the stricken look on her face.

To her intense mortification, she felt tears welling in her eyes. She thrust his coat at him. "You are right, sir, I don't— except for the obvious fact that you have taken an intense dislike to me. I shall endeavor to stay out of your way as much as possible for the rest of the trip." With as much dignity as she could muster, she turned to fetch her saddlebags.

"Oh, bloody hell," he muttered.

The inn was a shabby affair, small and run-down, like the rough dwellings they had passed since turning onto the rutted country road.

Davenport drew to a halt before they reached the unswept stable yard. "We shall be unlikely to meet any other travelers here," he remarked. "And it should be cheaper than along the main roads—though no doubt we shall be flea-beaten by morning." He turned to Caroline. Neither of them had spoken since their exchange of words some hours earlier. "Leave the talking to me. Contrary to what you might think, your voice does not sound in the least like that of a groom."

"I am not a complete idiot," she said stiffly. "My cousin also counseled me to keep mum."

He raised an eyebrow. "Then how did you expect to pull off the masquerade on your own?"

"I should have thought of something." She was silent for a moment. "I know, I could have feigned that an indisposition had robbed me of my voice—I would have had to whisper, and that I can do in a low tone."

He repressed a grin. "You are incorrigible."

"No, my lord. I am desperate."

When they dismounted, it took a few minutes before a gangly lad of no more than fourteen shuffled out from the stables to take the horses.

"See that they are properly rubbed down and fed," ordered the Earl as he handed over his reins. "There's a copper for you if you do."

That brought a glimmer of interest to the boy's slack face. "Awlright, mister, I'll take care 'a 'em good."

Davenport slung his bag over his shoulder. Caroline did the same. On reaching the door, he took firm hold of her arm. "Lean into me," he said in a low voice as they crossed the threshold. "And keep your head down."

Caroline needed little encouragement. She was exhausted, and his shoulder felt reassuringly solid and warm as she slumped against it.

The taproom was dark and smoke was already beginning to swirl in the fetid air, though only a handful of locals sat hunched over tankards of ale. The murmur of voices ceased as heads turned to look at the newcomers, but quickly picked up again when it became obvious they were of no interest. A wiry man of indeterminate age came around from behind the bar, taking in their nondescript clothing and dusty boots with a practiced eye. When the Earl asked for a night's lodging, he named a price and demanded payment in advance.

Davenport shrugged. "Show me the room—my groom is taken ill and needs to lie down." He straightened to his full height and his voice hardened with a tone of authority. "And make sure it is one where the sheets have been laundered in the last month."

The proprietor regarded him with a flicker of surprise, then grunted and bade them follow him up a set of rickety stairs. He pushed open the first door on the right. The room held two narrow bedstands. Squeezed up against the far wall was a simple pine dresser with a cracked mirror hanging slightly askew above it. The bedding, however, looked only marginally grey and the floor had recently been swept, though traces of dust still clung to the unwaxed boards.

After a quick glance around, the Earl dug for his purse and took out a few coins. "We'll want some supper," he said, handing them over. "I shall be down shortly. Have a tray ready for the lad. He'll take his up here."

The door closed. Caroline sank onto the nearest bed with a sigh of relief. Davenport tossed his bag on the other one, causing her head to come up with a start.

"Do you mean to . . . sleep here too?"

"We can hardly afford the extravagance of a second room. Besides, it would look deuced odd—a man does not hire a separate room for his groom." His back was to her and he was already placing his shaving things on the top of the dresser.

"But . . ."

"Oh, come, don't turn so missish. It is not as if you have never passed a night in the same chamber with a man. And I assure you, I am not as eager as your husband to use my fives on the opposite sex." He turned and caught a glimpse of her face, drained of all color. "You needn't fear any other . . . unwanted attention," he added quietly.

Caroline was too shocked to reply.

"I'll bring you your supper, then I'll have an ale downstairs while you ready yourself for . . . the night." He cleared his throat. "I took the liberty of adding a nightshirt along with the extra garments in your bag." With that, he left the room, closing the door firmly behind him.

She wished she could lock it in his wake—unfortunately, there was no such amenity gracing the rough pine. The color flooded back into her face at the thought of the Earl lying not four feet away from her for the entire night, clad in no more than a . . . First in words and now in deed, he seemed bent on humiliating her. She could not fathom why.

Her arms clutched the jacket tighter around her, as if to ward off a chill. The oilskin packet sewn in the lining pressed up against her chest. It reminded her that she must be strong, no matter what. She mustn't fail her father. With a sniff, she wiped away the tears that had formed at the corners of her eyes. It might not have been the wisest thing to allow the Earl to believe she was fleeing a rough husband, but since she dared not reveal the truth, she would have to keep up the charade. If that meant sharing the same bed-chamber with the insufferable man, then that was what she would do.

The door opened—he had not even had the courtesy to knock.

"I've brought you something to eat." He made a slight grimace. "As you might imagine, the choice was rather limited." A slice of cold mutton, rather grey around the edges, accompanied by a few slices of bread and piece of moldy cheese, sat on a chipped plate.

Caroline turned her head away. "I'm not hungry," she said, endeavoring to sound composed. "You may put it down anywhere."

He sat down next to her. Putting the tray aside, he reached for her chin and turned her face towards him. She tried to jerk out of his grasp but he wouldn't allow her to escape. To her dismay, there was still a trace of wetness on her cheeks. That only made her angrier.

"So, you do not intend to use force on me?" she cried. "Why is it that because you men are stronger, you feel you have the right to do as you please. . . ."

His hand dropped away, but his eyes held her with their piercing deep blue gaze. "If I could think of a way to spare your sensibilities, I would," he said quietly. "I hardly think it wise—or safe—for you to try to sleep in the stable. It is a rough crowd downstairs, and if it were discovered you were a female . . ." He let the sentence die. "And it is hardly possible for me to do so and let my groom stay here. It would attract undue attention, which I believe is exactly what you wish to avoid."

"My sensibilities," she repeated. "You have no idea what my feelings are, just as I have no understanding of yours— oh, damn it!" Another trickle had started down her cheek and she dashed it away with the sleeve of her coat. "I don't care that you hate me. Just get me to London. The sooner you do so, the sooner you shall have your money and be done with it."

Davenport reached into his pocket and took out a handkerchief. Without a word, he dabbed gently at the other cheek.

"I . . . never cry." She took a deep breath, furious with herself.

"I'm sure you do not."

She twisted from his reach. "Just leave me alone."

He rose and left without a word.

Chapter Five

The third ale still could not drown out the nagging of his conscience. Davenport knew he had been behaving very badly. He set the pint down with a thump and pushed away the unappealing supper, having lost his appetite as well.

Confound the chit. He sighed as he took another long draught. He had a right to be angry with her. After all, she had no business dragging him into her problems when he had more than enough of his own to deal with. It was not his fault that she had chosen a man who beat her, who wanted to batter down all independent thought and spirit, until she was no more than a hollow vessel, drained and empty. He stared at his own empty glass. Perhaps the fault wasn't his, but the choice ultimately had been. And something about the look in those bravely defiant eyes had made it impossible to turn away.

No, in all honesty it was not her weakness that angered him, it was his own.

He ordered another ale.

An involuntary smile stole across his lips. "Weakness" was the not the exact word for the exasperating young lady, he mused, as he recalled the past few days since she had stumbled into his life. She had faced pain and fatigue with more courage than most men. And her spirited defiance of his demands showed pluck to the bone. Why, even her recent tears had been no ploy to pull at his sympathy. The difference between this young lady who called herself Caroline and Helen was—no, he refused to dwell on such things. He drained the last dregs and rose. Damnation, let them both go to the devil. That was what they had chosen.

However he would endeavor to be more civil.

As the Earl made his way upstairs, a rough-hewn man seated in the dark recesses of the taproom sidled out of his chair and slipped out the door. It would be a long walk and the night was turning raw. But the reward would more than make up for any discomfort. After all, the flash cove had promised a guinea for a description of any travelers passing through the area. The man scratched at his stubbly chin. The tall, dark-haired fellow was easy enough—he had gotten a good look at him throughout the evening. The young groom was a more of a problem. He hadn't been able to see that one's face at all, or more than a hint of straw-colored hair from under the large cap. But at least he could give a fair picture of the lad's height and slight build. That should be enough—the toff couldn't expect him to paint a bloody portrait, now could he?

The cry so soft Davenport wasn't sure whether or not he had dreamed it. The second one, louder and sharper, brought him fully alert. The noise was going to rouse one of the other lodgers if it kept up. He slipped from his bed and went to kneel beside her. Her covers were in disarray, exposing her nightshirt to nearly the waist. The top buttons had come undone and Davenport couldn't help noticing that she looked—well, even less like a groom than before. Her hair spilled loosely over her shoulders, and one hand was gripping the folded jacket beneath her head, as if she feared that someone might want to make away with the ratty garment.

"I'm not afraid, Luce," she muttered. Her other hand was

clenched in a fist and the Earl took it between his own long fingers and tried to ease away the tension.

"It's all right," he said softly.

"No!" She sat bolt upright, her eyes betraying first fear, then confusion.

"It's all right," he repeated, taking gentle hold of her shoulders. "You were having a nightmare."

"Oh! I'm . . . sorry," she managed to reply as she struggled to gain control of her ragged breathing.

He could feel her still trembling through the thin fabric. Instead of returning to his own bed, he let his hands move to the back of her neck where they began to massage the knotted flesh. "Take a deep breath," he counseled.

All at once, the fight drained out of her and her head slumped forward, coming to rest on his shoulder. Without thinking, his hand came up to stroke lightly over the cascade of curls hiding her face. It was a few minutes before he spoke again.

"Better?"

She suddenly stiffened and pulled away, drawing the thin blanket up to cover the front of her nightshirt and looking away in embarrassment.

Davenport dropped his hands to his side but didn't move.

"I . . . I didn't mean to . . . disturb you. I won't let it happen again."

He ignored her words. "Would you like a glass of water?"

She shook her head. Her eyes were still averted.

"Miss," he began.

She started and turned towards him, as if to speak. But her eyes abruptly stopped at a spot somewhere below his chin, then widened in shock.

Puzzled, he followed her gaze down to his bare chest. He had retired clad only in his breeches—and usually he did without those. "Come now, it isn't as if you have never seen a man without his shirt on."

She continued to stare in fascination at the sight of the dark curls and the tanned skin, chiseled into taut planes by the days of manual labor.

"Ahhhem." He reached for where he had dropped his shirt and tugged it on.

Her head came up quickly. "You needn't concern yourself any longer, sir. I shall not bother you again." She made as if to lie back down, but he stopped her.

"Make sure it has passed before you try to sleep again."

She looked confused. "Why . . ."

"Do you have them often?"

"No. At least, not until recently," she replied truthfully.

He gave a short laugh. "I can't imagine why." Even in the faint moonlight she could see that his face held no edge of unkindness, that, in fact, his usual scowl had softened into something akin to a smile.

Her knees drew up under the meager bedcover and her arms wrapped tightly around them. "Would that the rest of this was only a nightmare as well, and that I could simply wake and find myself free of it all," she said with a heavy sigh.

"Mayhap that will be very soon," he replied softly. To his surprise, he found he cared more than he wished to admit that his words would prove true.

So the farmer hadn't been too deeply in his cups to make an accurate observation, noted the gentleman. He let the curtain of the carriage window fall closed and settled back against the soft leather. The hat might obscure the features and the jacket cover up the slender figure, but to an observant eye, nothing could hide the fact that the "groom" did not move quite like a lad.

No, there was no doubt. It had to be her.

But what was the chit up to? Who was the man with her and did he know what she was up to? That would add complications. . . .

Then his mouth curled upwards as he recognized her traveling companion. The Duke's daughter could not have chosen a less likely protector! It took little imagination to picture what the infamous Earl of Davenport was up to. How he had managed to strike up an acquaintance with the girl was still a mystery, but his intentions most certainly were not. He was known for his outrageous larks, especially when it came to seducing innocent young ladies. This masquerade had to have one purpose, and one purpose only.

Well, that suited his own purpose quite nicely. The dissolute nobleman would hardly interfere with his plans for the girl. No doubt he was already bored and, having ruined the chit, would be more than ready to move on to other entertainment. As to the girl's reputation, it was hardly of consequence. She would not live long enough for it to matter.

The gentleman rapped softly on the trap and spoke briefly with his coachman. The fellow nodded, then pulled the scarf at his neck up to his ears and stepped down to make a show of tending to the pair of matched bays.

Davenport and Caroline took their horses from the stable boy, who gave a whoop of delight at the coin tossed to him by the Earl. They mounted and rode out with hardly a glance at the carriage pulled off to the far side of the yard. With only a slight hesitation, Davenport passed by a rutted cart path and continued on to the main road.

They rode in silence, letting the horses have their heads, but the air of tension had eased, even though barely a handful of words had been exchanged since the night before. When the Earl reined his stallion to an easy trot, Caroline fell in beside him, content with the steady beat of the hooves as the only sound between them.

After a while, she ventured a question. "Where does this road lead?"

"It passes up through Salisbury, where we have a choice of routes to London. If we stayed on nothing but cart paths we could spend days meandering through the country-side—and for what purpose? It's more than likely we have already thrown off anyone seeking to follow us, so it seems in both of our interests to head to Town by the quickest possible way."

She nodded thoughtfully. "I think you are right."

"Good Lord, will wonders never cease" he replied dryly, though a flash of humor sparked in his eyes.

She turned to regard him with a serious countenance. "You think me a harridan, then?"

"I am not sure. . . ." His words were interrupted by the clatter of wheels as a sleek, well-sprung carriage drawn by a pair of matched bays flew by them.

Caroline stiffened in the saddle. "That carriage, it was at the inn this morning, I'm sure of it."

"No doubt it was. We are not the only travelers on the road, you know," reasoned Davenport. "There is no need to become upset over every carriage that happens to pass us."

"The occupant of that carriage did not spend the night at the inn—I neither saw nor heard anyone else moving about in any of the rooms," countered Caroline. "So why would it be stopped there at that hour? It doesn't make sense."

That gave the Earl pause for thought.

As they rounded a bend, they saw that a short distance up the road the carriage had pulled over and the coachman had dismounted to examine one of the front wheels.

Caroline drew in her breath, her hands gripping the reins until they were nearly white. The Earl took in her reaction, then reached around to remove something from his bag.

"It's all right. Continue on," he said quietly as he slipped the pistol into the pocket of his coat. Catching her eye on his movements, he smiled grimly. "I am not as complete a fool as you imagined. Naturally I wouldn't undertake a journey of this distance unarmed."

Caroline bit her lip and did as he bade.

As they approached the vehicle at a easy walk, the coachman suddenly straightened and shoved his hands into the pockets of his caped driving coat.

"Trouble?" inquired Davenport politely. He had placed himself between Caroline and the carriage, effectively shielding her from the view of anyone inside the vehicle.

With a snake-like move the coachman slid into the middle of the road, blocking their passage. At the same time, he drew a brace of pistols from his coat and signalled for them to halt. "Be on yer way, if ye knows wot's good for ye," he growled at the Earl. "Our business is with the girl." His eyes, half in shadow from the brim of his hat, darted to Caroline. "Get off the horse and get in the carriage."

Davenport made no move to ride on.

The coachman appeared momentarily disconcerted. "Go on, I tell ye," he said, waving one of the pistols at the Earl. "Stay out of this, or ye will be sorry. This don't concern ye."

"I fear you are mistaken," answered Davenport. "The girl is under my protection now."

The man gave a nasty laugh. "Oh, we've no doubt that ye have been sampling her pleasures all night, Lord Davenport. But I'm sure ye can find another willing female te warm yer sheets tonight. This one is ours, so be off."

Caroline didn't wait for the Earl's reply. She suddenly spurred her mount forward. The horse charged by the startled driver but it took him only a moment to recover from the surprise.

A shot rang out.

The horse pitched forward, then crumpled to the ground, sending Caroline sprawling in the dust. She dragged herself to her feet, clutching at the collar of her jacket. "You bastard," she cried. "You won't get what you're after."

Davenport hadn't moved a muscle save for the tightening of his jaw. His eyes went from Caroline, standing by the far side of the road, to the driver, whose second pistol was aimed straight at her heart.

"I believe you have the right of it. This is no concern of mine," he said slowly. "With your leave, I'll take myself off."

Caroline's lips curled into a sardonic smile. No words were needed to convey what she was thinking.

A head, masked in black silk, appeared from within the carriage. Wordlessly it nodded to the coachman.

The other man bared his teeth in a wolfish grin and turned back to the Earl. "Very smart, yer lordship. No female is worth the trouble—ye can always get another one." He motioned with the empty weapon. "Go on, then."

The Earl shrugged and set his stallion into an easy trot. For a brief moment, he passed between Caroline and the driver. The rest happened with blinding speed. In one motion, he drew his own pistol, whipped around and squeezed off a shot. At the same time, he leaned down, grabbed Caroline by the waist and urged the stallion into a full gallop. Another shot rent the air, but the horse didn't miss a step. Clinging low to the animal's neck, Davenport kept tight hold of Caroline, shielding her person with his broad shoulders. With a flick of the reins, he guided his horse off the road and towards a fallow field, guarded by a tall stone wall, overgrown with brambles. The stallion cleared it with ease and they disappeared from sight.

"Are you all right?"

The Earl pulled the big horse to a halt and set Caroline down on the ground. He slipped from the saddle as well, and with a pat to the lathered flanks, let the animal drink his fill from a small stream.

"Yes—a few more bruises hardly matter." She managed a game expression and brushed a lock of hair from her face, only adding to the streaks of dirt on her cheek. "I . . . that is . . . thank you, sir. You had no reason to take such a risk for me." There was a pause, then all at once she sank to the ground and drew her knees up to chest. "I had no right to involve you in this," she went on, her voice barely above a whisper. "That man was right. Leave while you can. You have done more than enough."

Davenport smiled faintly. "Ah, but then I should lose my thousand pounds."

Her head shot up in time to catch a glint of humor in his eye. "Don't be a fool—"

"I'm afraid it's far too late to correct that." He sat down beside her. "What have you done? Steal the family jewels?"

Her chin came to rest on her knees. "I can't tell you that either."

He regarded her thoughtfully.

Caroline sighed. "I don't know . . . who to trust," she said, half to herself.

One of the Earl's eyebrows came up slightly. "I see." His tone hardened. "Certainly not a fellow like me."

The color rose to her face. "It's not—you don't understand. It involves more than . . ." She gave up trying to explain and merely shook her head in mute confusion.

There was a long silence. Davenport picked up a small stone and skimmed it across the water, sending ripples out across the smooth surface from the point of impact. He appeared to have forgotten her presence, so intent was he on watching the spreading patterns. Then, abruptly, he spoke again.

"You now owe me for a horse as well as the other sum."

It was mention of the dead animal that finally brought tears to Caroline's eyes. "Poor beast," she said, trying to keep her voice from breaking. "I never meant for him to . . ."

"It won't do to dwell on it." Mentally chastising himself for being so inept, Davenport laid a hand on her arm. His voice sought to lighten the mood. "Come now, buck up your spirits. Surely you're not going to become missish on me over a small thing like someone trying to put a period to your existence?"

Caroline had to laugh in spite of herself. "Oh dear, if you put it that way . . ." She wiped at her cheek with the frayed cuff of her jacket. "Do you always see the absurd in a situation?"

He smiled lightly. "It is hard not to. The world can be a cruel enough place without a sense of humor to take the edge off it."

She regarded him intently. "You sound as if you have . . . suffered more than your share."

"Does that seem so—" He caught himself and fell silent for a moment. Recovering his equilibrium, he went on. "You are able to laugh as well, despite what you have been through. You have spirit, miss, whoever you are. I wouldn't have imagined until now that a young lady could show such fortitude—and wits."

Her expression remained thoughtful and it seemed to take a few moments for his words to register. "It seems we keep surprising each other. I wouldn't have imagined a reputed wastrel could show backbone or brains." She flashed a grin. "We are an odd pair, are we not, sir?"

Despite the mud and bruises, Davenport was struck by how bewitching she looked at that moment. It put him off balance and he merely grunted in order to hide his loss of composure.

"Why do you ladies put up with it?" he asked abruptly. "Why it is you are drawn to cruelty, then remain in thrall to it? I admit, I am at a loss to comprehend it."

Caroline stared at him, first with disbelief, then with a simmering anger. She had spent enough time tending to her father's tenants that she had seen something of the real world. More than one farmwife had sported bruises with a frightening regularity. Though there were always explanations of careless falls and the like, she hadn't missed the muttered talk among the other women about husbands who vented their frustrations with life on those unable to defend themselves in any way.

"You speak as if we have much of a choice," she said slowly. "Or perhaps you have conveniently forgotten that in our society those of my sex have no more rights than, say, a dog. We have no property, no recourse under the law—you men are free to treat us as you will with no fear of reprisals." Her voice rose. "You . . . own us as surely as you own your horse. And even if we run away, how do we exist without money? Even you can comprehend that! Then, what if there are children? Do you think any caring mother could abandon her offspring? For I'll remind you again, a woman has no right to her children! She cannot take them away from a violent man. How dare you speak of choice, my lord? It is hardly as simple as you suggest."

A look of shock, followed by a touch of embarrassment, crossed Davenport's face. "I . . . I hadn't thought of it quite like that," he admitted.

"I'm sure you hadn't," she replied, but her tone had become a trifle less sharp. "Perhaps in the future you will not be so quick to judge."

He looked away, his mouth pursed in a thoughtful expression. It was true. He had been angry with Helen for accepting what Charles did to her, but he had never really considered what her choices were. Run away? Caroline was right. Charles had the right to drag her back. Even if she were able to hide from him, how would she survive without resorting to a life as bad as the one she was leaving? His brows knitted together. Things were not as black and white as he wished to think.

"Do you have children?" he asked abruptly.

She shook her head.

After an awkward silence, Caroline cleared her throat. "I don't suppose they could follow us yet, but we had better decide what to do—assuming you really do mean to continue with me?"

"I told you, I need the blunt," he replied, but his tone softened the words. He seemed a bit relieved to have the subject changed. "Besides, my life had been sadly flat until you tumbled into it. Why, I only had to cope with angry creditors, sullen tenants and badgering tradesmen. Now I have the privilege of having someone try to shoot me."

She rose, wiping her hands on her tight-fitting breeches, and grinned again. "Have you any idea where we are and how we can reach London? I admit I am at a loss, for the moment, for any ideas."

"Somehow, I doubt that."

Caroline's eyes strayed to the big black stallion. "Surely Nero cannot carry both of us for long." She paused for a second. "Such a magnificent animal—he must be worth a handsome sum."

Davenport scrambled to his feet. "You've tried to steal him, you've nearly gotten him killed. Don't even think of trying to sell my horse." He took up the stallion's reins and gave him a fond pat on the neck. "Besides, it happens that I do have an idea."

Lucien Sheffield cast a harried glance at his uncle, whose countenance had gone nearly red with fury. "I daresay General Wilmott would dispatch a party of men to take us to the coast if it were at all possible, sir."

The Duke smacked his fist into his palm and muttered something under his breath.

Outside the tent another cannon boomed. The young Viscount began to pace up and down in the confined space. "May I ask why is it so important to get home?" he asked in a hesitant voice.

The Duke looked up, and for the first time his nephew could remember, there was a look of uncertainty, even helplessness, in the older man's eyes. "I fear that if we do not reach England right away, a number of people are going to be in grave danger—and the first one may be Caroline."

"Caro has used her wits to get out of more scrapes than you can imagine," answered Sheffield, with more bravado than he felt. "She is well able to take care of herself, Uncle Thomas—I can vouch for that."

"Would that I could believe that," he murmured. "You are not aware of all she is up against. It appears there is a traitor somewhere. . . ."

There was a sharp intake of breath.

"Yes, quite." The Duke pulled a face. "It wasn't until we landed in Brussels that I learned of the danger. By that time, a vital document was already on its way to me in England. Our adversary knows of it and its importance. I can only hope my own letter reached Roxbury Manor in time to keep Caroline well away from trouble. Whoever the traitor is, he is both cunning and ruthless."

"You . . . you think he would harm Caro?"

"I have no doubt of it, just as I have no doubt that Caro will not shirk from the danger."

Sheffield's hands balled into fists at his side. "Damnation. What can we do?"

"For the moment we can only pray, Lucien, we can only pray."

The gentleman ripped off the silken mask and tossed it onto the seat beside him. What the devil did the bloody Earl think he was about? Was the man completely foxed, even at this hour? Surely he wouldn't have risked his own neck out of any sense of honor or duty. That thought gave cause for his frown to deepen. His underlings were paid handsomely enough not to miss. This was the second time. It would not go unnoticed.

His silver-tipped walking stick tapped at the trap with more rather more force than necessary and he snarled a curt series of orders before falling back against the squabs. The carriage sprang forward. Time was of the essence, and he had now wasted far too much of it on playing cat and mouse with the chit.

He must have that document.

With an effort, he brought his temper under control. The two of them couldn't get far on one horse, and the big stallion was a fine enough piece of horseflesh to draw notice wherever they put up. With a grunt of satisfaction, he realized he had no real cause for concern. There was no way that they could slip through his net of informants.

She wouldn't elude his grasp next time—he would see to it himself.

Davenport tied the stallion inside the tiny mews and took Caroline by the arm. They made their way through a narrow alley and emerged on a small side street, in front of a narrow building, its timbers and stone darkened with age. A stout woman in a mobcap and voluminous apron that was once white answered the Earl's knock. Her eyes narrowed as she took in the appearance of the two rather disreputable-looking persons standing on the front steps. "Whatcha want?" she asked suspiciously.

"Is Mr. Leighton in his rooms?" inquired Davenport.

She hesitated. The voice was that of a gentleman despite the dirty and disheveled clothes. Though her expression indicated she had her doubts, she stepped aside and motioned up a set of narrow stairs. "Top floor."

They walked up four flights and knocked again at a warped door that strained against its flimsy latch. A muffled oath greeted the sound. There was a slight shuffling, the rattle of glasses and another low curse before it flung open, missing the Earl's nose by less than an inch.

"Well?" A mop of unruly brown hair hung over a high forehead, framing a slender, almost delicate face whose high cheekbones and pale complexion only added to the rather ethereal air about the figure. The dark hazel eyes, by far the most striking feature of the young man's visage, were narrowed in annoyance until they recognized the figure in front of them.

"Julian!" he exclaimed, laying aside a sable brush and absently wiping his hand on the front of a paint-spattered linen shirt. "Good Lord, what—"

Davenport took Caroline by the elbow and brushed past his friend, drawing the door shut behind them. "Sorry to intrude on you, Jeremy. I know how much you dislike being interrupted in your work."

Caroline found herself facing a large artist's canvas, resting precariously on a rickety easel. It depicted a landscape, with the sea in the background, rendered in a style of great originality and imagination. The light and colors were ethereal but dazzling, wrought with a passion and technical skill that took her breath away. "Oh," she said impulsively, "what a marvelous work!"

The Earl gave an involuntary smile. "I see you have gained a new admirer. Trust me, she is not easily moved to compliments."

His friend regarded Davenport's disheveled state, then the figure behind him, his eyes betraying confusion at the Earl's reference to gender, as well as Caroline's decidedly unmasculine voice and legs. "You aren't by any chance . . . foxed, are you, Julian?"

The Earl snorted in disgust. "You know me better than that—why do you ask such a stupid question?"

The young man's brows arched as he looked again at the figure behind Davenport. "She?" he repeated slowly.

"Oh, that. Perhaps we should sit down, Jeremy," advised Davenport. "I suppose explanations are in order."

The young man motioned towards a couple of simple pine chairs arranged around a small table at the back of the cramped room. It was then that Caroline realized he had only one hand. His other arm ended in a stump shortly below the elbow and the shirtsleeve was rolled up and pinned closed to keep from flapping in the slight breeze that blew through the window. With a look that conveyed his acute embarrassment, he made a bit of room among several stacks of leather-bound books and took a seat on the edge of a narrow wooden bench.

"Sorry," he mumbled, staring at the floor with an expression Caroline found endearing. "I rarely . . . entertain."

That elicited a laugh from the Earl. "To say the least." He glanced around at the cluttered space, crammed with rolls of linen, bottles of linseed oil, pigments and jars bristling with a variety of brushes in all shapes and sizes. In one corner, a group of finished paintings were carefully slotted into a wooden rack. "You have been busy, I see."

Jeremy nodded. "Thanks to your help, Julian, I . . ."

The Earl cut him off. "I'm afraid I have a favor to ask of you."

The young man's eyes lit up. "Anything."

Davenport repressed a smile. "Perhaps you should wait until you hear what it is."

For the first time, the other man smiled. It made his boyish face look even younger, though Caroline hadn't missed the fine lines etched around his eyes and mouth that denoted laughter was not the dominant form of expression for Mr. Leighton.

"It doesn't matter, Julian. Surely you know that."

"First of all, can you take care of Nero for a short time?"

The other man nodded, slightly mystified.

"We shall also need to find some clothes for Miss—the young lady here. And I shall have to ask to borrow a small sum"—he glanced pointedly at Caroline—"which shall be repaid shortly."

As Jeremy looked only more puzzled, the Earl sighed and proceeded to give his friend a brief summary of what had occurred over the last few days.

At the end of the explanation, the young man gave a low whistle and slanted an appraising look at Caroline, mixed with more than a touch of curiosity. He opened his mouth as if to speak, then hesitated, and turned back to Davenport instead. "I fear I'm not terribly plump in the pocket at the moment, but you are welcome to what I have. As for clothing, what sort of, er, garments do you need?" Again, his eyes strayed to Caroline and her all too visible legs.

Davenport gave a short laugh. "A good question." He cocked his brow inquiringly at her.

"Even though it will no longer fool whoever is . . . pursuing me, it may be easier for us if I remain dressed as a man," she replied. "We will be able to move about with greater freedom."

"I have a . . . friend who has a younger brother. I believe he is about the, er, right size." Jeremy blushed slightly at the intimation that he had taken note of Caroline's measurements.

"Perhaps you might visit Miss Fathing now and see if we might avail ourselves of some spare things."

The young man's color deepened.

Davenport's eyes twinkled in gentle amusement at his friend's discomfiture. "Come, put on your jacket. I'll go out with you." He turned to Caroline. "Will you be all right alone for a short while? I'll pick up a few things for supper and see about any coaches passing tonight in the direction of Salisbury."

She nodded.

He rose and made for the door. After a few steps he paused, drew out the pistol from the folds of his coat and placed it on the edge of a small table crowded with bladders of paint. "Do you know how to use it?"

Caroline's chin rose slightly. "I shoot nearly as well as I ride."

His mouth twitched at the corners. "Then I pity the poor fellow who comes unbidden through that door. I see we must have a care, Jeremy, on returning home."

"If you are tired, miss, there is a . . . that is, in the other room . . . I'm afraid it is not fit for a female but—"

"How very kind of you, Mr. Leighton," she interrupted. "I assure you, it will be very welcome indeed." The warmth of her smile caused the young man's shoulders to relax. He even managed a semblance of a smile in return. With that, the two men left, closing the door firmly behind them.

She lay down on the narrow bed for a short time, but even though she ached for rest, she was too agitated to sleep. After tossing and turning she gave up and, pulling her jacket tighter around her shoulders, wandered back out into the young man's workplace. The clutter was deceiving. On closer inspection it was clear that every color, every brush had its place, and that most things were organized on the right side of a table or easel, in easy reach of that hand. Her gaze went again to the large painting that dominated the small space, and once more she was startled by the sheer power of its emotion. The young man might be shy of speech but he had another form of expression perhaps more eloquent than any words could be. She studied it with a knowledgeable eye, being well acquainted with the works of many of the leading artists of the day. There was no doubt this young man was a prodigious talent.

On a low table in front of the narrow windows was a stack of sketchbooks. She couldn't resist the temptation to view more of his work. Seating herself in one of the simple pine chairs, she began to leaf through them. The pages were filled with bold charcoal sketches that caused her eyes to widen in admiration. A single tree, drooping with the weight of a summer rain, a heron picking its way along a riverbank, neck held crooked at just such an angle—Mr. Leighton had an uncanny eye for detail.

The next book held not only vignettes of the countryside but of people as well. There, with a fishing pole on his shoulder, head turned in profile, was a familiar face. The artist had captured the intensity of his gaze, the exact curl of his lips, the brooding look that rarely cleared from his brow. But who was the lovely lady walking beside him . . . ?

Someone gave a slight gasp.

"Oh!" Caroline's head came up with a start and color began to suffuse her features as she encountered Jeremy Leighton's astonished stare. She let the cover fall closed. "Forgive me for being so rude as to look at your drawings uninvited." She smiled tentatively. "I couldn't help it—your work is marvelous. Really."

The young man's shoulders relaxed slightly but he was clearly uncomfortable with praise. "Thank you," he mumbled, his gaze sliding to the floor.

She beckoned to the seat beside her. "Will you show me the rest of the drawings? That way, I'll not feel so ragmannered."

When Jeremy didn't move, she let the books drop in her lap. "I'm sorry. I didn't mean to offend you."

He dropped the rough bundle of clothes he had tucked under his bad arm and came over to sit next to her. "No, please. Don't think such a thing, miss. It's just that . . . I suppose I have lost my manners, living alone," he said haltingly.

"Well then, perhaps we two churls may enjoy each other's company without worrying about the niceties of Polite Society. And please, my name is Caroline." She grinned and was heartened to see a ghost of a smile come to his own lips. Taking up the sketchbook she had been perusing, she opened it at the beginning. After turning through the first few pages with him, she paused and asked if he were acquainted with the work of a minor artist who had recently caused a stir at the Academy with his style.

Jeremy's eyes lit with interest. "You are familiar with his work?"

She nodded and they began an animated discussion of the other man's merits. By the time the page turned open to the sketch of Davenport, Jeremy had lost most of his reticence.

"You have captured his lordship's . . . intensity very well," remarked Caroline. "Do you paint portraits as well?"

"Occasionally. But I prefer landscapes. People are too much trouble."

She wondered at the deliberate ambiguity of his answer, but forebore to comment on it. Instead she pointed at the delicate rendering of the lady. "Who is that beside Lord Davenport?"

"Oh, that's Lady Atherton."

Caroline's eyes lifted from the likeness. "The Earl is married, then?" For some reason, the thought bothered her more than she cared to admit. Of course he was, she reminded herself. Hadn't Mrs. Collins already intimated such a thing? How was it that the thought of it had seemed to slip her mind . . . ?

"Julian? Good Lord, no. That is his brother, the late Earl's wife." Jeremy hesitated for a moment. "Though I sometimes think it was Julian who was in lo—"

The door banged closed with a rattle. Davenport stalked across the room and placed a jug of cider and a package wrapped in oilskin down on the table with more force than was necessary.

"Have neither of you anything better to do than gaze at pictures?" he snapped. His eyes, so stormy they appeared nearly as charcoal as the lines in Jeremy's drawings, turned to Caroline. "I thought you had a modicum of concern about reaching London in one piece. It appears Jeremy has found some new garments for you, so why are you dallying about instead of trying to make yourself halfway presentable? Lord knows, you couldn't look any worse," he added acidly, raking over her muddy cheeks and disheveled hair with a withering look.

"Julian!" exclaimed Jeremy in a shocked tone.

"Don't be angry with Mr. Leighton, sir. He found me stealing a look at his sketches and I asked that he be kind enough to allow me to continue. There is no need to get in such a pucker over it." She couldn't help but add, "It is no wonder you are taken with her—she's quite beautiful."

Davenport's hand slammed down on the rough wood. "That's enough from you," he said through gritted teeth.

She regarded him calmly. "Indeed, I am now beginning to see the resemblance. You are looking nearly as nasty as that painting of you that hangs over your mantel."

A choked laugh caused both of them to turn towards Jeremy. "She's right, you know," he said. "Right now you *are* taking on an unfortunate resemblance to Charles." As Davenport glowered, Jeremy smiled at Caroline. "How astute of you, Miss Caroline. Most people wouldn't notice anything but the handsome face, but I—well, call it my little revenge on Charles."

Caroline's brows came together in confusion. "I don't understand. The man in the painting . . ."

"Is Julian's older brother—older by ten minutes."

"How long has he been . . ."

"Four months."

Comprehension slowly dawned on her face. "Good Lord," she whispered. "Then you are not him. You are *not* the Earl of Davenport. I mean, you are—but you are not."

"Ah, well." A note of irony tinged his voice. "It would appear that neither of us is what we seem."

Chapter Six

The Earl turned on his heel and retreated to the adjoining room, slamming the door shut behind him.

"I hope I have not put you in his lordship's bad graces." She cast an aggrieved look towards the locked chamber. "I vow, he is the most ill-tempered, high-handed, exasperating gentleman I have ever met."

Jeremy's brows came together. "Julian? You have the wrong of it, Miss Caroline. He is the most steadfast, generous . . ." He paused and looked discomfited, as if feeling disloyal in discussing his friend behind his back. In a low voice he added, "I pray you make allowances for his behavior. He has been under considerable strain these past months."

It was Caroline who felt a stab of guilt. No matter how shabby his manners, the Earl had risked his life to rescue her this morning. He was being well paid for it, she reminded herself, but that still did not quell the feeling that somehow it was she who was showing to disadvantage. Arrogant and mercurial though he might be, there was also no question as to his courage or quick wits. What a maddeningly complex man. That only piqued her curiosity more.

"How do you know his lordship?" she asked.

"We became acquainted at Oxford. Though Julian is several years my senior, we found we shared mutual interests." Lest she imagine the worst, he hastily added, "That is, we enjoyed discussing books and paintings." Again he halted, as if debating whether to go on.

Caroline laid a hand on his arm. "If you would rather not discuss it—I seem to be oversetting everyone today."

He gave a ghost of a smile. "On the contrary. You are remarkably easy to talk to. I find that I . . . don't mind. Like Julian, I am a second son as well, though of a mere baronet. Through family connections, my father wished for me to enter the Navy as a career—a less likely match I cannot imagine! But my father is not one given to reason. He could never understand why I didn't love to hunt and shoot and carouse." As Caroline watched his sensitive face harden at the memory, she could not but wonder at how blind a man could be to the true inclinations of his progeny. "It was only grudgingly that I was allowed to enter university. When I began to paint, it was outside of enough. Only Julian encouraged me to continue." He let out a harsh sigh. When he continued, his voice became even softer. "Then after the accident . . . well, my family simply disowned me. I imagine a man-milliner of a painter—and a crippled one at that— was simply too much for them to bear."

Caroline's eyes brimmed with sympathy. "How terrible for you," she whispered.

"It is not for your pity that I am telling you this. It is so you understand what sort of a man Julian is."

"I didn't mean to sound—"

"It is only through his generosity that I am able to survive on my own and continue my work, though I know he can ill afford it. I suppose he feels in some way responsible for what happened. He has always tried to make amends for Charles."

"His brother was the cause of your accident?"

Jeremy's mouth quirked. "Charles never gave a thought to whether his pranks caused harm to anyone. In fact, he never gave a thought to anyone save himself. The world is well rid of him. Perhaps Julian will now be able to find some peace. . . ."

The sound of the door opening caused him to stop abruptly.

Davenport came back into the room. He had washed the worst of the dust from his person and had brushed his garments so that they looked passably neat. His face was rigidly composed and when he spoke, his voice was under taut control once again.

"I suggest you change," he said curtly to Caroline, gesturing to the bedchamber.

She rose, took up the bundle of clothes that Jeremy had let fall to the floor and went into the other room without a word.

"And you, I would appreciate it if you would leave me out of your fanciful conversations," he continued to his friend.

"I'm sorry, Julian, but I didn't wish her to have the wrong impression—you *have* been acting quite the bear, you know. It isn't like you."

"I don't give a damn what she thinks of me," he growled. "I am doing this for the blunt."

Jeremy didn't answer but regarded Davenport with a penetrating stare.

The Earl turned from the scrutiny and made a show of cutting a hunk of cheese from the package he had brought in with him. "A mail coach passes through in an hour. With luck, I shall return in a few days and you shall not have to worry for pigments or canvas for some time."

"I cannot bear being such a burden . . ."

Davenport clapped him on the shoulder. "It's merely a loan—you shall repay me after you have exhibited at the Academy and have to turn away commissions."

Jeremy shook his head. "The Academy—would that my work would ever hang there! But I have no connections, no influence. There is not a chance."

"We'll see."

Caroline reemerged, dressed in a looser set of breeches that hid her shape better than the old ones, as well as a clean shirt. Her hair had been regathered and tucked up under a thick wool cap.

"Was there not another jacket?" demanded the Earl.

Caroline clutched the old garment around her person. "I prefer this one."

He eyed it with distaste but merely shrugged. "I suggest you eat something. We must leave shortly." Without bothering to note whether she heeded his advice, he turned and picked up the jug of cider, then let it thump back to the table with a grunt of disgust.

"I don't suppose you have any brandy?" he growled.

When Jeremy shook his head, Davenport ran his hand through his freshly combed locks, undoing his careful efforts, and went to stand by the window, his back towards the room, his gaze riveted somewhere in the distance.

He stayed there, unmoving, until he announced it was time to go.

Jeremy took up his coat too. "I'll come with you," he said as he followed them down the stairs. "I think it would be wise if I showed you a way to the inn that avoids the streets, where someone might observe you passing."

Davenport looked as if to argue, but then seemed to sense how much his friend wished to be of help. "Very well."

They threaded their way through a series of darkened alleyways. The sun had nearly set and the air had taken on a distinct chill. It promised to be an uncomfortable passage to Salisbury, thought Caroline as she quickened her steps to keep pace with the two men ahead of her. But at least she would have plenty of time to think on all that Jeremy Leighton had revealed during—

She was nearly jerked off her feet as an arm snaked around her neck and pulled her into an adjoining passageway. "Lookee what I have here," rasped a low voice that she nonetheless recognized as that of the coachman from the mysterious carriage. "What a stroke of luck to have ye stumble across my path." The cold barrel of a pistol pressed against her temple. "Quiet!" he snarled, cutting off her cry of surprise. "Ye nearly cost me my position this morning. Well, ye won't get away this time."

The sound of hurried steps caused the man's head to turn. "Stay where ye are," he warned as Davenport and Jeremy drew to a halt in front of him. "None of yer bloody tricks this time. Get off with ye or the girl will pay."

Caroline started to speak but the man struck her across the mouth. "Shut up!"

Davenport's jaw tightened but his hand caught Jeremy square in the chest, restraining his friend's charge towards the other man. He shoved the young man back towards the way they had come. "You heard him, Leighton. There's nothing more we can do."

The coachman waited until they had disappeared in the gloom and the echo of their footsteps grew faint against the grimy bricks. With a satisfied smirk he tightened his grip on Caroline's coat and forced her to start moving.

"Julian!" protested Jeremy as soon as they had rounded the corner.

"Quiet," hissed Davenport. He pushed his friend forward. "Show me where that passageway comes out. Quickly, man!"

Without hesitation, Jeremy broke into a lope and guided them between a row of decaying wooden houses, avoiding the piles of garbage strewn around their feet and the snapping jaws of a roving mongrel. In a short time, after more than a few twists and turns, Jeremy pointed to a dark gap between low warehouses. Davenport nodded and pressed his finger to his lips. Signalling Jeremy to move away into the shadows, he took up position to one side of the opening and drew his own pistol.

Within moments, the scrabbling of boots over loose stones gave an indication that someone was moving towards them from the inky depths of the passageway. Caroline stumbled out first, the man's hand still firmly clasped at her neck. The pistol had come away from her head but still pressed menacingly at the small of her back. That caused Davenport to pause for an instant. Then as the coachman emerged from the darkness, the Earl's hand snaked out, wrenching the man's gun up and away from Caroline.

A shot rang out.

With a muffled oath, Davenport pried the weapon from the other man's grasp and let it drop to the ground. The other man, no stranger to fisticuffs, recovered with astonishing speed. Pushing Caroline to the ground, his booted foot lashed out in a vicious kick, catching the Earl on the knee and sending him staggering. A chopping blow sent Davenport's pistol skittering under a jumble of hogsheads.

Both men began circling each other.

"Want a beating to that pretty face o' yers?" sneered the coachman, feinting to the right. "I'll be happy to oblige. When I finish with ye, yer own doxy won't recognize ye." With a bob of his head, he sought an opening, but the Earl hadn't been fooled. "I see the snivelin' cripple has run off," he taunted. "Not that 'e be any use te ye."

Davenport parried a wicked left, then countered with a hard shot that caught the man square on the nose. As blood spurted out, the man gave a roar of pain and lunged straight ahead, knocking the Earl back into the wall. His beefy fist came up, poised to deliver a punishing blow, when suddenly a length of stout hickory came down on his head. Reeling from the unexpected impact, he staggered a step or two until a lashing punch to the jaw from Davenport laid him out cold.

"Likes to hit people until they hit back," muttered the Earl from between clenched teeth. He looked up at the slight figure brandishing a section of broken axle in one hand. "Well done, Jeremy. My thanks."

"My lord, you are hurt!" Caroline had picked herself up from the mud and was staring at the dark stain spreading at Davenport's shoulder.

"It's nought but a scratch," he replied. "Come, that shot will have a crowd here at any moment. We must be away."

Jeremy threw down his makeshift cudgel. "Follow me."

Caroline lit the lantern and held it close to the unconscious form of the Earl. "Is he . . ."

"He's fainted." Jeremy looked up uncertainly. "The wound doesn't look too bad. But there is quite a lot of blood."

Caroline untucked her shirt and began tearing the long tails into strips. "I know a bit about tending to injuries." She knelt down beside him and carefully peeled Davenport's coat and shirt back from his injured shoulder. With a sharp intake of breath, she pulled the Earl's shirttails out as well and ripped a goodly amount of fabric from them. "I fear the shirt was ruined anyway," she said wryly as she folded the material into a thick compress and pressed it hard against the ragged gash.

But in truth, the heavy bleeding had her worried. After a few minutes, she used the strips she had torn to bind the pad to the wound, then looked over to Jeremy. "He needs to be properly attended to, but I'm afraid that your rooms are no longer safe. Is there somewhere we may take him, somewhere away from this town? Though how we shall manage to move him . . ."

Jeremy gestured towards the small gig standing beside them. "Can you harness a horse?"

She nodded.

"A lady of many talents." He flashed a smile as he brushed the straw from his breeches and stood up. "Old Patch is as docile as they come. I am acquainted with the owner and when he learns of the circumstances, I doubt he shall be overly angry if we . . . borrow his conveyance for a short while."

He went to fetch the animal from a stall at the back of the small stable while Caroline began to wrestle with a tangle of harness hung from a wooden peg. Jeremy pulled a face as he watched her drag it down and nimbly sort out the straps and reins.

"What a helpless idiot I am," he muttered.

She slanted him a look as she began to fit the horse's bridle. "You are only an idiot if you truly believe that. Rather than mourn for what you don't have, you should feel very fortunate to possess such a rare talent as you do. You are luckier by far than most people." Her fingers quickly did up the last few buckles and tightened a strap or two. "Besides," she added, "I saw what you did. Hardly helpless—Gentleman Jack himself couldn't have landed a better blow."

Her words caused his brow to furrow slightly. He stood silently, as if deep in thought, as she backed the animal into the traces and finished making things ready. It was only when she hesitated and asked his aid in moving the Earl's prostrate form into the back of the gig that he snapped out of his reverie and rushed over to help. Together they somehow managed to lift him up into the pile of straw covering the rough boards. Caroline added an old horse blanket she spied hanging from the door of a stall. Though hardly in a pristine state, it would help in warding off the chill.

Jeremy had taken up an old stovepipe hat sitting atop a

pile of discarded burlap bags and planted it firmly over his curling locks. It came down to nearly his eyes and she would have been wont to giggle if he hadn't looked so resolute.

"I can drive a gig," he announced, his tone almost daring her to challenge his assertion. "I do it quite often. You should lie down in back with Julian with the blanket drawn up over you both until we pass out of town. It is less likely anyone will take note of a poor farmer in a simple gig." He turned the collar of his coat up to heighten the effect.

Caroline had to agree it was a good plan. She took her place under the musty wool, stifling the urge to sneeze at the cloud of dust and horsehair that mizzled over her head and shoulders. At least the smell wasn't unbearably rank. Jeremy slid the door of the stable open and checked that all was clear.

With a flick of the reins, they were off.

The gentleman watched from the shadows as a small group of men gathered around the man lying in the mud. As he was helped to his feet, blood streaming from his broken nose, voices demanded to know what had happened.

"Thieves," croaked the coachman. "I was merely stretching my legs after a day of driving when suddenly I was set upon by three of 'em. Armed they was, too. But I managed to fight them off."

A murmur of consternation ran through the group.

"Thieves? We don't countenance such goings-on here. Did you happen to get a good look at them?"

"Aye. One was a tall, well-built fellow with a scar on his cheek, another was kinda skinny, hardly more than a boy, and the third was a cripple—missing his left hand, he was."

"Why, that sounds like Mr. Leighton," cried one of the tradesman who had rushed out from a nearby tavern at the sound of the shot. "But I cannot believe that such a gentleman would be involved in this."

"He's a bit queer in the head," muttered another man. "Roaming around the countryside with his paints and such."

As the group helped the coachman back towards the inn, the gentleman slipped from his spot and hurried away. Damn his man, he had bungled things yet again. The trap had been sprung before things were in place, and now the quarry was at large again. His fingers curled around the butt of his own silver-chased pistol, itching to put it to use. He would pay a call on Mr. Leighton, but he doubted that he would find anyone there. He would have to set to casting his net in a wider direction and hope that it pulled in something—and soon. His polished boots hurried along the uneven cobblestones.

Time was running out.

It could have been worse, she thought, as the gig hit yet another rut. If the vehicle was able to travel at more than a plodding walk, the jarring would no doubt be even more noticeable. As it was, the comfort was tolerable but the sedate pace set her teeth on edge. Would she never make any progress towards London?

Yet another bump caused the Earl's leg to bounce and press up against hers. She could feel the solid contours of his muscled thigh, the heat emanating from beneath the snug buckskins. It was disconcerting, yet oddly comforting. There was no move on her part to pull away. In fact, her arm reached out to cradle his shoulders as it occurred to her that the jostling could be doing no good for his wound. She shifted even closer to him, settling his head on her chest. His breathing was slightly labored but there was no sign of fever on his brow. Unconsciously, she brushed the dark locks back, letting her fingers linger on the smooth skin. In repose, the planes of his face were softer, more vulnerable than he ever allowed them to appear when awake. Still, the signs of worry and strain were visible in the lines etched around his eyes, in the set of his lips.

With a swallow, Caroline realized she had only added to them. Even yesterday, the thought of it wouldn't have upset her greatly. Now, she found she cared a great deal. Rather than add to his burdens, she wished she could help ease them. She wished she could keep the laughter and the lightness she had glimpsed in his quixotic eyes from being chased away by the black moods that blew in quicker and heavier than storm clouds.

His breath tickled her throat with the gossamer lightness of a summer breeze. Stormy yet capable of great gentleness. She tightened her arm around him. There was so much to think about in regards to the Earl—if only she could keep her eyes open.

Davenport awoke with the strangest feeling that a horse was sitting on his head—a bizarre dream, no doubt! Still muzzy with sleep, he shifted slightly to banish the odd sensation. The soft warmth beneath his cheek was no figment of his imagination, however. It felt quite pleasant and he had no desire to do away with it. With a deep sigh of contentment, he burrowed his head deeper. His hand also came up to seek out the heat, closing lightly over a tantalizing mound of . . .

"Oh!"

Davenport's eyes flew open in confusion. His hand slid away from Caroline's chest and he started to sit up.

Caroline's arm restrained him. "Don't try to move, my lord. I fear you may open your wound."

He was suddenly aware of the sharp throbbing in his shoulder, the jostling of the gig and the prickle of hay under his coat. "What happened? Where the devil are we?"

"You've been shot," she replied. "You fainted, then Mr. Leighton and I carried you to a stable and, well, we have borrowed a gig and are taking you somewhere safe where you can be properly looked after."

"Fainted?" he muttered. "Only females faint—where are we going?"

Caroline repressed a grin. "I meant, sir, that you passed out from loss of blood. As to where we are going, I don't know."

His finger probed gingerly at his injury. "It's been bandaged. How . . ."

"I managed to stop the bleeding, though I fear that both of our shirts are quite the worse for it." She slid up into a sitting position so that his shoulders rested in her lap and his head remained cradled on her chest. Her arms remained wrapped around him in a protective manner. "But truly, you must stop moving about. Please try to get some more rest."

It was a novel experience, someone fussing over him, caring about his own well-being. He found he had no inclination to disobey her order to stay still. He was quite comfortable where he was. His eyes were on the verge of closing when he noticed the cut on her mouth. Instead, they narrowed in consternation.

"Damnation, he struck you."

"Yes, well, I suppose another cut hardly matters, does it?" Her tongue ran lightly over the split in her lip. To his consternation, the fleeting gesture sent a frisson through his limbs.

Caroline tugged the blanket up higher. "Are you chilled, my lord?"

He merely grunted, looking away to hide the flare of desire he was sure would be evident in them. His senses must be addled from shock, he thought. There was no other explanation.

"You have real backbone, Miss Caroline," he said softly, finally managing to take control of his thoughts.

She swallowed, trying to quell the strange sensation in the pit of her stomach. It was the first time he had spoken her name. For some reason, it made her feel rather giddy.

"It's quite easy to appear brave when someone is always coming to the rescue. Once again you had to—how did you put it?—scrape me out of the mud. It must be getting very tiresome."

He mumbled something under his breath.

"I'm sorry to have put you to so much trouble," she continued. "Dear me, it seems to keep getting worse."

Davenport chuckled at that. "Worse? Let me see, I've been engaged in a mad chase on horseback, I've been shot at, punched and now winged. I figure at this rate I shall be sticking my spoon in the wall by tomorrow."

"No! I—" Her voice caught in her throat.

"Here now, I was merely teasing. Don't let me overset you." Was it his imagination, or had her hand brushed up against his cheek in something akin to a caress?

"Hmmph. Well, it's no joking matter."

He didn't answer. But when he closed his eyes, there was a slight smile on his lips.

Caroline awoke to the palest glimmerings of dawn on the horizon. With a stab of guilt, she sat up, careful not to disturb the sleeping Earl. The gig was moving at a faster clip, she noted with satisfaction, but poor Mr. Leighton had been driving for hours. He must be exhausted.

"Mr. Leighton," she called softly. "Forgive me—I fear I have abandoned you all night. Surely you need some sleep yourself. I could take the reins for a time."

Jeremy turned his head. He did look a bit peaked, but there was also a glimmer of satisfaction in his eyes. "No need. We will be there shortly. And actually, I find I have enjoyed the task. It is rather novel to be able to partake in an adventure again." His eyes shifted to the lump next to Caroline. "I take it Julian has not suffered a turn for the worse?"

"He seems to be resting comfortably enough, but I think

his wound should be properly cleaned and bandaged soon lest a fever set in."

"Yes, well, that won't be a problem. But let us hope that it is his temper that does not become inflamed. I'm afraid he won't be overly happy with our destination, but I couldn't think of where else to go."

Caroline wondered what he meant, but Jeremy seemed loath to continue. With a shake of the reins, he turned his attention back to the road and began whistling a lively country melody.

The air had taken on a tang of salt. They must be near the sea, she thought, as she leaned back in the hay and stared up at the fading stars. The question was, had she managed to come any closer to London, and how would she continue? Perhaps wherever it was they were going, there would be a carriage, a horse—anything. She let out a little sigh. Despite his growls and snaps, she would miss the reassuring strength of the Earl's presence, for surely he would have had enough by now. Indeed, she had. She wouldn't allow him to risk his person any longer. No, from now on, she was back on her own.

Davenport stirred. His eyes fluttered open, then narrowed as they took in the lightening sky. "How long have I been asleep?" he demanded.

"Hours. But Mr. Leighton says we are nearly there."

"Where?" His head was still resting on Caroline's lap.

She shook her head. "That he has not told me."

"Jeremy," he called out. "Where are you taking us?"

There was a long silence.

"Jeremy?"

After a slight hesitation, it seemed the younger man decided it was wiser to give in to the inevitable. With a resigned shrug, he finally answered, "To Lymington."

Davenport's brows came together. "Who do you know in Lymington?"

"Lady Helen."

The Earl shot up, wincing at the pain that shot through his shoulder. "The devil we are!" he roared as he started to get to his feet. "I—"

Caroline's hand caught him full in the chest. Off balance, he fell back in the hay.

Mr. Leighton then spoke up. "Julian, there was really no other choice. We needed a place where you can get some attention for your wound, and I didn't think we could have risked anywhere close to town. I am sorry if it does not meet with your approval, but in truth, it is the perfect place—it's quite isolated and away from prying eyes. It will give us a chance to decide how to proceed."

Davenport looked to argue but Caroline fixed him with a glare. "If you so much as twitch, sir, I shall be forced to act again. You heard Mr. Leighton. His reasoning makes sense." The beautiful, delicate lady in Jeremy's drawing came to mind, and she found herself wondering why the Earl should be disturbed about the prospect of ending up on her doorstep anyway. How romantic, she thought a bit acidly, to arrive bloodstained and heroic, in need of help from one's beloved. Lady Helen would be his for the taking.

She found herself taking a distinct dislike to Lady Helen.

He glowered at her, but other than a few choice words muttered under his breath, he remained silent.

The gig turned onto a long, winding drive that carried them through a stand of ancient beech and elm. At the crest of a hill was a modest stone manor house overlooking a rocky inlet. Jeremy pulled the exhausted animal to a halt in the courtyard and an elderly groom shuffled out from the stable to eye the vehicle with a mixture of curiosity and surprise.

Davenport climbed down stiffly from the back, brushing wisps of straw from his rumpled coat. "Kindly inform Lady Artherton that she has some visitors, Davis."

The man stated openmouthed at the disheveled figure before him until it suddenly dawned on him who it was. "Y-yes, Mist—er, my lord. Right away." His head bobbed and he scurried away.

"Oh, devil take it, we might as well wait inside," muttered the Earl. He stalked towards the entrance, trailing the other two in his wake.

Not waiting for a servant to answer his knock, he yanked the massive oak door open and entered. The entrance hall had recently received a thorough going-over. The woodwork gleamed from a fresh coat of wax, the rugs looked newly beaten and a duster had been run over every possible surface, including the single ornately carved picture frame that dominated the wall opposite the curved staircase. Fresh flowers stood on the mahogany side table.

A man Caroline took to be the butler stepped forward. His carefully schooled features betrayed no hint of emotion about the odd little party in front of him. "My lord, I have sent word to her ladyship of your arrival. If you would care to wait in the—"

"Julian!" There was a rustle of silk above them, and a slender figure appeared around the curve of the banister. The lady paused for a moment, her hand flying in a gesture of surprise to her alabaster throat, then she rushed down the remaining stairs. "Dear heavens, what has happened?"

"I apologize for intruding on you in such an unseemly manner—"

"It's my fault, really, Lady Helen," interrupted Jeremy. "You see, we had a—"

"Have you basilicum powder, hot water and clean linen?" Caroline was in no mood to let the two men stumble through long-winded explanations. The Earl was looking decidedly pale beneath all the dust and she didn't like the look of the new splotch spreading out from the rent in his coat.

Lady Helen turned. She took in the figure before her, from the muddy boots, ragged breeches and torn shirt to the long strands of honey-gold hair that had come loose and now dangled lower than the shoulders. Her mouth fell open in shock. It took a moment to recover her wits. "I . . . I imagine so. Mrs. Dawkins would know . . ."

"Then let us ask her right away."

Lady Helen looked confused, then nodded at the butler, who hurried off.

Davenport shot an reproachful look at Caroline, then continued. "I'm afraid we've gotten into a bit of a scrape. I'm sorry that Jeremy saw fit to come to you, but now that we are here, perhaps we might clean ourselves up and have a bit of breakfast."

"Julian, you know I would be glad to do anything to help." Her hand came up to rest on his arm. It was then that she noticed the damage to his coat. "Why, you are hurt!"

"Just a scratch," he muttered.

Lady Helen shrank back. "Oh, but there is . . . blood. Shall I send for a doctor? Or perhaps Mrs. Dawkins knows what to do."

"A doctor may not be necessary. I believe I can attend to his lordship, if you will show us a room where he might lie down."

The butler reappeared, followed by the housekeeper bearing a large tray holding all of the items Caroline had requested. Lady Helen seemed to breathe a sigh of relief. "Dawkins, please take his lordship right up to the bedchamber overlooking the garden." She faltered, then added, "And perhaps his . . . friend would like to make use of the one next to mine."

As everyone moved towards the stairs, Lady Helen held Jeremy back. "Who is that . . . urchin with Julian?" she whispered in his ear.

"It's rather a long story."

*   *   *

Viscount Sheffield reined his horse to a halt and stared in frustration at the raging waters.

"Lucien!"

"Over here, Uncle," he called out. With a last, helpless look at the swollen river, he spurred his mount back towards the group of riders waiting on the crest of the hill.

"I'm afraid there's no chance of crossing here," he reported. "The currents are much too strong."

The Duke's face became even grimmer.

A portly Austrian officer accompanying their detachment began to speak in fractured English, drawing puzzled looks all around. After a slight pause, one of the young adjutants cleared his throat and ventured to speak. "Your Grace, if I understand correctly, the major says that he recalls there is a small bridge not more than a few miles downriver. The rains may not have washed it out."

The Duke waved an arm at the foreigner. "Well, man, what are you waiting for? Lead on!"

The young Viscount fell in beside his uncle. "I've consulted the map with Lieutenant St. John, and once we cross the river it is not more than half a day's ride to the road to Ostend. God willing, we should reach the coast by sometime tomorrow."

The Duke merely nodded, his eyes remaining riveted straight ahead. Lucien did not miss, however, the subtle clenching of the jaw or the fact that the powerful hands tightened convulsively on the reins.

He started to speak again, then thought better of it. He had never seen his uncle reduced to such a state. The Duke was a man of intimidating presence, whose stoic demeanor might be taken as cold unless one were on intimate terms with him. And even then, there was a certain aloofness to his manner. It was not always easy to know where one stood with him, mused Lucien. At times, he was almost sure His Grace thought him the verriest of fools, a jackanape to be tolerated only for reasons of blood. In fact, he was of the opinion that Caroline felt much the same—

Caroline. The thought of the danger she was in caused his expression to mirror that of his uncle. He knew quite well what her reaction to danger would be, and it brought forth a string of silent oaths that would have put a Jack Tar to blush. If only there were someone she could turn to for help. The very thought of such a thing caused his mouth to quirk into a rueful smile. Lord, she was nearly as stubborn as he was, and the chance that she would admit she couldn't handle things on her own seemed well nigh impossible. After all, she had never done so to anyone but him.

Who, in all honesty, was capable of helping her?

Lucien gripped his own reins harder and slanted a side-long look at the Duke, wondering if it was just such thoughts that were occupying the other man's mind as well.

Who, indeed?

He set his spurs into his mount's flanks, causing the horse to bolt forward towards the head of the column. Suddenly he understood his uncle's overwhelming sense of urgency. And the look of fear on his face. The two of them were all she had.

Caroline peeled back the torn fabric and cut through the ragged strips of fabric wrapped around Davenport's shoulder. She frowned at the sight of the jagged cut, then took up a moistened sponge.

"Ouch!"

"Sorry. But it must be done." She bent back to the task. It actually cleaned up rather nicely, and in the light of day, didn't look half so bad as she had feared. After probing gently in a few spots, she was satisfied no further ministrations were necessary. A liberal dusting of basilicum powder finished things off and she began to tear the clean length of linen into bandages.

The Earl had worn a scowl through the entire process. "Don't know why females have to make such a fuss over a scratch."

"A gunshot wound is hardly a thing to treat lightly, sir," she replied tartly as she wound the last strip into place. "There. Now mayhap you'll stop growling like a bear at everyone. Perhaps that will also serve to improve your disposition."

The Earl made as if to protest, then his jaw snapped shut. He took in the dark smudges under her eyes, the sag of her shoulders. "Will you promise me you will lie down and get some rest?" he said quietly.

She nodded, fighting to keep from pitching forward smack into his bare chest.

A knock at the door announced the arrival of the butler. He carried in a large tray and the scents of grilled bacon, eggs, kippered herring, toast and strong, steaming tea filled the room. He was followed by two maids struggling with a hip bath that they placed behind a screen in the corner.

"I took the liberty of having Lady Helen's butler bring you a full breakfast. You must be famished by now. He's also going to try and find you a fresh shirt at least. And I thought you might like a bath."

She started to rise but Davenport held her arm for a moment. He seemed to be searching for the right words.

"Thank you."

She nodded again, not trusting her voice, then left his room.

True to her word, she immediately went to the bedchamber Lady Helen had offered. Without removing any of her clothes, she sank into the blissful softness of the thick eiderdown cover. Her sigh of pleasure turned into a groan, however, as a soft knock came at the door.

Lady Helen came into the room. "Forgive me for disturbing you." Her arms clutched at a thick dressing gown. "I thought perhaps you might also wish a hot bath. I've told the maids to bring a tub here as well. And I brought you something to change into while they give your garments a good cleaning."

"That's very kind of you."

Lady Helen approached the bed. "Jeremy and I have had a long coze. He has told me something of what has happened." She drew a deep breath. "I wish to help you in any way I can."

Caroline was taken by surprise, both by the words and the depth of passion beneath them.

"I have a carriage, I have money. You have only to name what you need."

The offer was more than generous, especially coming from an utter stranger. Caroline blinked. "Lady Atherton, I hardly know what to say—"

"Please call me Helen. And you needn't say anything. Just get yourself free of the monster who has done that to your face." Her lips compressed. "I didn't have your courage, but at least I may help another of my sex escape from an unconscionable tyranny."

A flush stole up over Caroline's features. It suddenly became very clear to her what Lady Helen's life had been like as wife to the late Earl of Davenport. And however passive her own role had been in letting certain assumptions be made, she felt terribly guilty at eliciting such profound emotions under false pretenses.

Lady Helen misunderstood the cause of her discomfiture. "Forgive me if I speak of things that are still too raw to contemplate. But be assured, you will find the will to face them. Take strength from the support of loyal friends. It isn't necessary—or possible—to do it alone."

"There are different types of courage, Lady . . . Helen. Somehow I doubt that you are as lacking in that quality as you claim."

The other lady smiled tentatively. "But no doubt you think me a veritable featherhead from my performance this morning. I fear I am reduced to acting as if I didn't have any wits about me when Julian is present."

Caroline closed her eyes. Though her opinion of Lady Helen had altered considerably, she was in no mood to share any confessions of girlish rapture.

"You see, though he doesn't think I realize it, I know I have taken from him that which I had no right to take. I am immeasurably better for it, though he, most certainly, is not. It wasn't until very recently that I came to understand it all, and understand how difficult it is for him to forgive me—and himself. I only wish I could let him know in some way that I comprehend why. Perhaps it would help him get on with his own life. And perhaps we could truly be friends. But I fear that I can't ever seem to find the right words—they simply tumble out all wrong and I end up making a goose of myself."

It was not at all what Caroline had expected to hear.

"So it makes for an awkward situation." She sighed. "I'm not quite sure why I am telling you this, except Jeremy seemed to think it might . . . matter to you."

Caroline's blush deepened. "I don't know why he . . . that is, I cannot imagine . . ."

She was saved from the need of further speech by the arrival of the tub and two young maids bearing pots of hot water. Lady Helen left her to her bath, and as she shed her garments, it seemed that her spirits felt a certain weight lifted from them as well.

Scalded, scrubbed, enveloped in a clean, sweet-smelling gown, she had barely laid her head upon the pillow, precious jacket tucked safely beneath it, before her swirling thoughts gave way to a deep, impenetrable slumber.

Chapter Seven

Davenport woke slowly, savoring the crispness of the sheets, the feel of the pressed linen against his soaped skin, the gentle support of the feathered pillow and thick horsehair mattress. It was all one could wish for. Yet in the muzzy state between sleep and consciousness, he was oddly aware that he would rather be lying with his limbs stretched out on a pile of straw, his head resting on a pair of shapely thighs. . . . He came sharply to his senses.

Where was she? Was she all right?

The thought caused him to sit up and swing his bare legs out from beneath the warmth of the covers. His clothes, freshly laundered and free of the scent of stable and straw, hung over a chair. A new shirt had been found to replace the ruined one. He dressed quickly, noting that aside from a touch of stiffness, his shoulder didn't hamper his movements in the least. When she didn't reply to the knock on her door, he hesitated for a moment, then let himself into her chamber.

She was asleep. Her hair, still damp from her bath, fanned out over the pillow, the sunlight catching glints of gold and copper. He had to restrain the urge to brush the stray tendrils from her cheek and the corner of her mouth. The dressing gown had parted slightly to reveal a deep notch of creamy skin. At that moment she looked almost fragile, and undeniably feminine. His mouth quirked slightly at the thought of breeches and boots. He found himself wondering what she would look like in an elegant gown cut low and slim to flatter her willowy form, her hair artfully dressed to highlight her expressive features. . . .

She stirred, her hands moving restlessly up to the pillow to catch at the ragged jacket folded under its downy bulk. Slender hands, yet so capable—throwing a credible shot to his nose, handling the reins of his stallion, tending his injured shoulder and now guarding that rag of a garment. Good Lord, she seemed to cling to it like some sort of talisman, but if it brought her some modicum of comfort, he supposed there was no harm in it. With a long sigh, he reached down and gently pulled the quilt back up to cover her, then slipped from the room.

Lady Helen and Jeremy were in the drawing room. The young man was still taut with nervous energy, though he hadn't appeared to have slept, and his eyes had a gleam to them that caused the Earl to smile inwardly. The adventure seemed to be doing his friend a world of good.

Davenport helped himself to a cup of tea and a piece of toast. There was a long silence as he ate, then he moved to the tall mullioned windows and gazed out over the sea.

Jeremy shifted from foot to foot, impatient with his friend's reticence, until finally he could bear it no longer. "Julian," he exclaimed. "Have you decided what we should do?"

"We?" repeated the Earl. "What *you* are going to do is take the gig and return to Sway."

Jeremy's face took on an expression as stubborn as that of their other companion.

His tone softened somewhat. "Have you forgotten that at the very least, Nero needs looking after? You have done more than your share in helping us out of this coil. Rest assured that I shall see Miss Caroline safely to her destination."

"I think I have some sort of say in that, my lord."

She was dressed as a lad again, save for that her hair was

still loose, simply swept back to fall behind her shoulders. The others had turned at the sound of her voice, but Davenport remained facing the window, hands clasped behind his back, his expression inscrutable.

"Julian wishes to pack me off back home, life a helpless child," muttered Jeremy as he cast a dark look at the Earl.

"Well, on that, at least, I'm in agreement with him." At the sight of his injured expression, she smiled sympathetically. "There is the matter of the gig, too. We can't have the Runners after you, can we?" She refrained from adding that on no account would she risk exposing the stalwart young man to any further physical danger.

"Oh, very well," he conceded. "I suppose you may be right. We don't want Bow Street becoming involved."

"How do you mean to go on?" asked Lady Helen. "Do you wish to take my carriage?"

Caroline considered the matter. She glanced at Davenport, but he gave no indication of paying the least heed to the conversation. "It appears my nemesis has quite a network of informants along the roads," she began. Her brow furrowed. "Hmmm."

It was Lady Helen who thought of it first. "I daresay this is a wild notion, but there is a small sailing boat moored in the cove. One of the tenant farmers uses it on occasion to fetch supplies from Portsmouth. I don't suppose you know how to—"

"Enough!" exploded Davenport. "Pray, don't be giving her any more harebrained schemes than she manages to come up with on her own."

Caroline found herself almost missing his words, so intent was she on observing his face as he turned to look at Lady Helen. Her stomach gave a little lurch.

So it was true. He wasn't in love with her.

"But, Julian," protested Jeremy, "it's not harebrained at all! With all the fleet activity, there must be hundreds of small craft around the harbor. And with all the sailors and supplies and official dispatches, not to speak of the rest of the town, it would be impossible for anyone to keep a careful watch on all the traffic coming and going. Slipping unremarked onto a coach to London should not be difficult at all."

"It hardly matters what his lordship thinks." Caroline had regained a measure of control over her thoughts. "He isn't coming, regardless of what means I choose to use." Her chin came up a fraction. "And you needn't worry about the money, sir. I will see that you receive the full amount for what you have already done."

Davenport's eyes took on the distinct color she had come to recognize as a signal for a storm. But instead of answering her, he took up a bottle of brandy from the sideboard and stalked from the room without a word.

The door closed with a resounding bang.

The three of them exchanged uncomfortable looks.

"Dear me," murmured Lady Helen. "Julian never loses control of himself. Since when has he developed such a temper?"

"Since he met me," answered Caroline with a sigh.

The other lady choked back what sounded like laughter. "How wonderful," she managed to say.

Caroline's brows drew together in puzzlement.

"One is only indifferent if one doesn't care." Seeing that the import of her words still hadn't dawned on Caroline, she merely smiled.

Jeremy looked thoughtful, then shrugged and changed the subject. "What shall you do?"

"I mean to think on it—but not on an empty stomach. Forgive me if I seem rude, but may I ask for a tray to be sent up to my room? I need some time by myself to sort things out."

*   *   *

It was finally quiet throughout the house. Jeremy had lately been settled in a room down the corridor with the admonition to get some rest. The Earl was apparently nursing his wounds, physical and otherwise, with the bottle within the confines of his own chamber. After sending Cook herself up with enough food to last for days, Lady Helen had stopped by briefly to ask if there was anything she could do, but Caroline has assured her that all was fine for the moment.

A short while later, a small package was delivered to her room by one of the maids. The purse was reassuringly heavy, noted Caroline as she stood by her window and watched Lady Helen walk off with the gardener to confer on what was to be done with a bower of overgrown roses. At least one worry was taken care of, judging by the glint of gold as she slipped the bulging leather purse into her jacket pocket.

A cursory look showed that the hallway was empty. Caroline wrapped a portion of the remaining food in a large napkin, then debated on whether to leave any sort of note. What possible scribble could adequately convey her feelings? Better to leave things unsaid rather than said badly. She trusted they would understand. Later, she would make amends for her actions.

If there was a later.

She hesitated only a fraction before the Earl's door then moved resolutely on, down the stairs and out the French doors of the music room. A gravel path, bordered by tall privet hedges, led through a formal garden and down towards the cove. She had to slow her steps as it changed to a mere trail through rocks and gnarled roots. But the way was clear enough and soon, just as Lady Helen had described, she spied a small craft tied up to a narrow wooden jetty.

As she came closer, Caroline surveyed it with mounting satisfaction. It was obviously tended with care. The rigging was taut and showed no signs of wear, the hull looked well caulked and the sail was neatly furled around the varnished spar. She had sailed on numerous occasions with her cousin in a boat similar to this one, though never by herself. Still, she had little doubt as to whether she could handle it on her own. . . .

"Ah, I had expected you a trifle sooner."

Mouth agape, she spun around at the sound of the familiar baritone.

Davenport was lounging against a stack of wooden crates. He eyed the bulging napkin tucked under her arm. "Stopped for nuncheon, I see. But you should have inquired as to the tide. There is little time to spare."

By now her jaw had assumed its proper place. "What are *you* doing here?"

"Really now, I've come to expect more rational questions from you. I, too, have an engagement in London, if you will recall."

"You are foxed!"

He held the bottle up to the light and made a show of gauging its contents. "I must be, to contemplate doing what I'm doing. And in all fairness, an extended time in your company could drive even a saint to drink."

"I'm not taking you with me! I thought I made that clear."

He rose and shoved the bottle in his pocket. "As for *you* taking *me*—well, I suppose we might see who would prevail in a battle for the boat, but I daresay we can't afford to squabble." He began casting off the lines. "If you have any nautical sense whatsoever, you will mark those clouds to the east and take my meaning." Jumping lightly onto the deck, he turned to her.

"Well, are you coming?"

The gentleman's patience was nearing an end. The ebony walking stick drummed with a rising degree of force against the side of his immaculately polished boot. He re-crossed his legs, then flicked at a minute speck of dust sullying the sleeve of his coat. Finally, there was the sound of footsteps approaching the carriage and the curtained door was opened a fraction.

He regarded the face that appeared with a look of disgust. "Have you managed to discover anything useful?"

The other man touched nervously at his mottled nose as he shook his head. "No, my lord. Still no sign. But they can't have disappeared into thin air. Someone will spot them soon." He cleared his throat. "The only thing out of the ordinary is a gig has been reported as missing, but I have word that it was seen heading southwest, in the direction of New Milton or Lymington. Do you wish . . ."

The point of the walking stick pushed the man back a step. "Drive on to the next inn, you fool," snarled the gentleman.

As the coach sprang forward, he sank back against the squabs and considered what to do. Even with the considerable raise in reward, none of his informants had been able to ferret out the whereabouts of the damnable chit. A visit to the rooms of Mr. Leighton had turned up signs that she had been there, but it had proved fruitless in determining where she might have gone.

His hand came up to stroke his smoothly shaven chin. If she didn't turn up in the next hour or two, he couldn't afford to chase about any longer. He had an alternative, of course. He always did. The stick began to rise and fall again. He had hoped to avoid putting it into action—admittedly, the risk was far greater. But at least it would leave nothing to chance.

The waves began kicking up into whitecaps as soon as they left the shelter of the cove. Low, scudding clouds darkened the horizon around the Isle of Wight, hinting at a stiffening wind and perhaps some rain.

"Can you take the tiller for a moment?" called Davenport as he surveyed the spread of canvas. "I think it might be wise to put a reef in the mainsail, just to be safe."

Caroline moved from where she had just finished belaying the jib sheet to take over the steering. The Earl watched her movements with grudging approval. "It's a good thing you were not exaggerating your experience in a boat. I fear we are in for a bit of a blow."

She squinted at the craggy shoreline. "Are there any charts below? How shall we navigate to Portsmouth?"

"If we stay within sight of land, it will not be a problem. But if we can't make it by dusk, it would be best to put up somewhere for the night."

A frown creased her features. "Why don't we leave the sail as it is, then? We shall make better time."

She stood straight up at the stern, head tilted back, chin thrust forward into the teeth of the oncoming weather. The wind was blowing straight in her face, and her hair, which she hadn't bothered to pin back under the man's cap as yet, streamed out past her shoulders like the flying colors of naval frigate. Flecks of spray clung to her cheeks, and her eyes had a dogged sparkle to them not due entirely to the beads of water. In response to a sudden gust, her hand instinctively eased up on the tiller so the boat did not lose way. Davenport found himself grinning in spite of himself—she looked every bit as resolute as a post captain at the helm of a ship of the line.

"It may get wet," he warned, for already the lee rail was nearly buried in the foaming water.

"I'd rather be wet than delayed yet again."

"Very well." And he took another turn of the mainsheet.

A few hours later, Caroline was close to regretting her words. Not only was she soaked with spray but the temperature had dropped considerably so she was chilled to the bone as well. Her bare fingers were so stiff they could scarcely manage to work the lines that the Earl had sent her scrambling to loosen, and the combination of salt and rough hemp had rubbed them raw. Still, she voiced no complaint. They were fairly flying across the churning sea. Surely Portsmouth could not be far off.

"Are you all right?"

Her jaw wouldn't seem to obey her command to speak. The words came out as a mere croak.

Davenport motioned for her to return to the shelter of the cockpit. She crawled awkwardly back across the slick deck and took a seat beside him. At the sight of her shivering limbs, his mouth compressed in a tight line, but just as he was beginning to speak, a sudden squall caught them from astern. The force of the wind knocked the mast nearly horizontal with the churning seas, sending Caroline sprawling towards the lee gunwale. Only the Earl's strong grasp saved her from disappearing beneath the foaming waters. As it was, her left side was soaked to the skin, setting her teeth to chattering uncontrollably.

Just as suddenly, the wind died, the sky took on a less ominous hue and the seas became calmer. Davenport threw a leg over the tiller to keep on course then took Caroline's hands between his and began chafing them. She closed her eyes as the warmth started to seep back into her extremities. Without quite knowing how it happened, when she opened her eyes she found her head was settling on his shoulder.

"Oh!" She straightened and made a show of brushing the hair back from her cheeks. "Sorry."

He shrugged out of his coat and draped it over her shoulders.

"No, please. You'll catch a chill yourself, sir."

"Nay, the wind has dropped."

He noted that she was still shivering slightly and his arm stole around her and pulled her closer. As he did, there was the muffled clink against the varnished wood. He reached into the pocket of the outer garment and extracted the bottle of brandy.

"Here, a swallow of this will help warm you."

She looked askance, first at the bottle and then at him. "I'm not sure if that is a good idea, my lord. The last time was not a pleasant experience—for either of us."

Davenport chuckled. "I shall refrain from pouring half the bottle down your throat in this instance." He took a swig himself and then held it out to her.

After a moment's hesitation, she accepted and tentatively let a small taste pass her lips. A sharp cough nearly sent it back from where it came. Her face puckered. "It does set fire to your innards, does it not," she muttered as she passed the bottle back.

The Earl merely grunted and placed it back in her hands.

The second sip was not nearly so bad. In fact, she decided that, like so many other things, brandy was something rather nice that men had conspired to keep to themselves. A pleasant tingling began to replace the numbing cold in her limbs. She sighed and slumped even more heavily against the solid warmth of the Earl's body. A smile drifted to her face as she listened to the wind in the rigging and the rush of water against the hull. "What a sail—it was quite exhilarating, was it not?"

He chuckled again. "Does nothing dampen your spirits?"

She grinned as drops of spray beaded on her face and shimmered in her hair. "Every other part of me seems to be soaked, but my spirit? I'm afraid I'm a bit like a dog with a bone in his teeth on that regard. I don't give up very easily."

His mouth quirked slightly. "So I have seen. But at least you will allow that it was not such a bad idea in consenting to let me come along for the ride. You might have landed in the suds—quite literally—had you attempted this on your own."

She colored. "I am not such a slowtop as to think I could have managed as well by myself, sir. I didn't want you to come not because I would prefer to be alone but rather because I didn't want to put you in danger any longer—you were nearly killed last night on my account and I cannot . . . I won't allow it."

Davenport shifted uncomfortably in his seat. The idea that she was thinking of his welfare caught him off guard. "I'm being well paid for it, remember?" he said gruffly. "It is in my own best interest to see you reach London—I have desperate need of that money."

"I see." Her voice changed imperceptibly. "Well, rest assured that when we land, you may take yourself off and I shall still send you the full amount. You have certainly earned it."

He cursed inwardly at his own clumsiness. "I didn't mean—" He cut off his words with an exasperated shake of his head. "You know, you are quite unlike any female I have ever met before."

Her expression became unreadable. "Yes, I suppose I lack the delicate sensibilities that those of my sex are supposed to exhibit in order to please Society and attract a gentleman. I'm afraid I've never been very good at falling in a faint or succumbing to a fit of vapors when trouble arises. No doubt that is one of the reasons I shall have little luck in finding a . . ." She stopped short. "Well, it is one of the reasons my cousin has pronounced me an incorrigible hoyden."

Davenport mulled over her words while taking another drink. He found his curiosity was piqued for he thought he had finally discerned the root of her troubles. "You speak frequently of this cousin of yours. Were you forced into a marriage you didn't want? Is it he you are in love with, rather than your husband? Is that whom you are fleeing to?"

"I should be well glad if Luc—if my cousin is in London, but I fear he won't be." Her expression turned contemplative as she studied her hands for the longest while. The Earl had just about decided that no further words would be forthcoming when she spoke again.

"As for being in love with him—of course I love him. He has been like an older brother to me throughout our childhood. But I cannot imaging having anything but sisterly affection for him. Certainly not the sort of love you are referring to."

"Whom are you running to, then? And whom are you running from?"

She didn't answer this time. Instead, her eyes seem to seek out a point way off on the horizon. He remained silent as well, the tight line of his mouth the only indication of his less than sunny mood. His left hand took over the steering again, while the right one set to helping the brandy disappear at a good clip. On nearing the bottom of the bottle he offered her a final shot.

"Well, here's to both of us making it to London in one piece—with the way things have been going I suppose the outcome is still very much in doubt."

Caroline roused herself from her reverie and downed a goodly mouthful. "Oh, I don't doubt it at all," she said. Then she promptly fell asleep against his shoulder.

His mouth softened into a grudging smile. He had meant what he had said—she was truly unlike any other female of his acquaintance. Such was her spirit and her pluck that he imagined most people would fail to notice an unmistakable vulnerability about her as well, despite her show of bravado. A glance down at her face, unguarded in repose, showed a bewitching mixture of strength and need. One thing was certain. She was utterly wrong about what was all that attracted a gentleman's attention. . . .

He steered his thoughts away from those dangerous waters. It was best he remember why he was here—as he had said, he needed the money.

The thought of his recent words made him grimace. How the devil had he managed to throw her concern for him back in her face in such a churlish way? With a sigh, he had to acknowledge to himself that it wasn't the first time he had shown to disadvantage. His behavior had, for the most part, been less than gentlemanly since he had met her. No wonder she thought him an ill-tempered dog. Or was it a bear? In either case, he discovered he didn't like the notion one bit.

But the fact that she found him disagreeable hadn't prevented her from having a concern for his person. It puzzled him. Despite the dire threat to her own safety, her thoughts had turned to how she could shield him from further danger. Not to speak of how she had tended to his wound, cradled him through the jolts of the long journey and then cleaned and stitched the jagged flesh before seeing to her own needs. It was almost as if she . . . cared. But then, in a trice, her tongue could turn from soothing to scathing.

Maybe it was the brandy or the fatigue or the dull ache of the gash in his shoulder, but it all seemed terribly confusing. Rapacious creditors, sullen tenants, fallow fields—they were all problems he could face without a qualm, he thought glumly. But a certain young lady seemed to be oversetting his carefully constructed world. There was nothing for it except to put all questions regarding the maddening little urchin aside until a later time.

Perhaps at some point he could make some sense of it all.

The afternoon was fading rapidly. The storm clouds had given way to high, billowing heralds of good weather which were beginning to take on rich pink and orange hues of sunset. In the distance, a massive ship of the line tacked into view, its towering square sails almost blinding in the golden light.

He hesitated a moment before gently nudging Caroline out of her slumber, somehow loath to let go of the comfortable intimacy between them.

"Where are . . ." she mumbled, still muzzy with sleep.

"We are nearly at Portsmouth—look ahead."

She sat up, blinking in surprise at the sight of the four-decker hoving a line towards the Lizard.

"Quite awesome, isn't it? Let us hope our Navy can help put an end to the Little Corsican and all the bloodshed and destruction his visions of grandeur have caused."

"You have no sympathy for the Emperor? Many people on the Continent have welcomed his return with open arms."

His brow creased. "I cannot imagine any rational person being gulled into believing the man cares for aught but personal glory. And at what cost? The sooner he is stopped, the better—but then, I imagine neither politics nor Napoleon are paramount in your thoughts."

Caroline made a sound in her throat that might have been taken for acquiescence.

As they came nearer the entrance to the harbor the number of vessels increased dramatically. Luggers loaded with supplies plied the waters under the bows of merchant ships setting out for the Atlantic and several frigates flying the ensign of the Channel Fleet.

"Best fix your hair," advised Davenport as he kept a sharp watch on the ships around them.

Caroline found her cap and with a few deft twists quickly arranged her long locks to fit snugly under the thick wool. There was no further conversation as the Earl had to navigate a series of rapid tacks to avoid collision with a squadron of two-deckers taking advantage of the ebb tide.

Her hands were recovered enough to handle the sheets without mishap, and their craft made its way safely into the midst of the bustling port.

Davenport chose to put in at a dock where over a score of burly sailors was engaged in wrestling a cargo of barrels loaded with salt pork up the gangplank of a barge. Amid the curses, the grumblings and the harried admonitions of the young lieutenant in charge, no one took note of the small vessel dropping sail on the far side of the pilings or its two nondescript occupants. The Earl made sure the canvas was neatly furled and the mooring lines securely fastened to the massive iron cleats before taking Caroline by the elbow and hustling her towards the alleyway between a ship's chandlery and a sail-maker's loft. Her first steps were somewhat unsteady, causing his grip to tighten.

"Steady," he hissed in her ear. "Walk smartly now. The less attention we attract, the better." He gave a quick glance around. "And let us hope the press-gangs are not out tonight," he added under his breath. That would entail a good deal of explaining that he would dearly like to avoid.

"Stop yanking me about. I'm quite capable of making my own way," she muttered back, though in truth she was still feeling a trifle light-headed from the spirits. "In fact, you can—"

He shook her into silence as they emerged from the alley into a busier cobbled street. A group of men staggered past them, singing an extremely bawdy song and laughing uproariously as they struggled to remember all of the verses. Caroline managed to pay rapt attention until they were out of earshot.

"What is a sodomite?" she whispered to Davenport. "And how does he—

"Never mind!" snapped the Earl as he gave her arm another shake.

"Ouch!"

He let go of her. "For the love of God, keep your head down. And turn the collar of your jacket up."

They were passing under the glow of a gaslight outside a tavern. The noise coming from within its smoky confines gave evidence that the place was not lacking in either clientele or high spirits. Davenport paused after they passed into the shadows.

"I shall have to inquire of someone from which inn the coaches depart for London." His hand came up to rub along the scar on his cheek as he contemplated what to do. At that moment, two gentlemen emerged from the tavern and turned in their direction.

"Hell and damnation," swore the Earl. "It is Lord Hartford. He's bound to recognize me, and given that our nemesis knows my name, that is something I would very much like to avoid."

"Well, *do* something, then," whispered Caroline, though even as she said it, she realized she was being unfair. What could he possibly do at a moment's notice?

Davenport muttered something under his breath, then suddenly grabbed her around the waist and crushed her to his chest. His lips came down on hers, hard at first, then softening as if he, too, were as surprised by his actions as she was.

Her first impulse was to pull away. But for some reason, after the initial shock she merely tilted her head back in order to voice a protest.

"Hush," he murmured as his lips left hers for a moment. "Trust me—they will quickly depart."

His mouth was back against hers in the next instant, before she could manage a single syllable, and his tongue was brushing her lips in a manner that was most intriguing. The sensation sent a jolt of heat through her, as potent as the earlier taste of brandy, and nearly as intoxicating. It was utterly unlike any of the few kisses she had allowed an admirer to steal during a walk in the garden. Those had been, at heart, rather silly affairs.

There was nothing silly about the Earl's embrace. As she made to speak again, his tongue slid into her mouth. He tasted rather exotic, a mixture of fiery spirits and the tang of the sea. She found herself nearly overcome by the new sensation, and without thinking, wound her arms around his neck to steady herself. His own hands slipped down to the small of her back, molding her to his own lean form.

Somehow, she was aware that the footsteps coming towards them had stopped.

"What the devil . . ." sputtered a voice, disgust evident through the slur of drink.

"Call out the watch," exclaimed the other man. "The filthy scoundrels should be clapped in irons and thrown in the gaol." His head wagged back and forth. "Unnatural, it is. Unnatural."

Out of the corner of her eye, Caroline saw them retreat a few paces, then turn and hurry off in the opposite direction. She let her head fall away from the Earl's. A little gulp of air cleared her thoughts enough for her to speak.

"I . . . I think they are gone."

"Mmmm." His lips traced a path along the curve of her jaw. "Are they?"

It was another moment before he slowly released her. Shaken, she drew back a step or two and began to fiddle with her cap, which had fallen sadly askew. Though her clothes were still uncomfortably damp and the chill in the night air had deepened, she felt hot all over. The darkness, she hoped, would cover the fact that her face must be several shades redder than normal. That the Earl appeared totally unaffected by what had just transpired did not help her composure in the least. But at last she gathered her wits enough to speak coherently.

"Ah . . . very clever of you, my lord—but how did you guess such an . . . action would drive them away?"

He shrugged. "It was not a guess. Any proper gentleman would have been put to flight by that little display of depravity."

"Depravity?" she repeated faintly.

"I am referring to the spectacle of two men engaged in an intimate act."

"But—oh, I see." She looked confused. "Surely two men wouldn't ever . . ."

Davenport took her firmly by the arm. "Perhaps your dear cousin will explain it to you at some later date—I most certainly will not." He started marching her away from the harbor.

"But . . ."

"Kindly refrain from any further questions. Your garments may fool most eyes at night, but your voice will not fadge, especially among this sort of crowd," he growled.

It was only through a concerted effort that she forced herself to swallow a retort and did as she was bade, or so she told herself. In truth, she was having a hard enough time just concentrating on putting one foot in front of the other to think of something scathing.

The Duke grasped the gunwales of the lurching ship to keep from being tossed across the rainswept deck. Next to him, the young Viscount turned up the collar of his borrowed oilskin and shouted to be heard over the groaning of the rigging and the snap of wet canvas.

"The captain thinks the weather should break in another hour or two. Then he should be able to set us back on course."

His uncle merely drummed his palms against the varnished rail and stared out into the roiling blackness. The wind had increased to near gale force, and all around them, men were scurrying up the ratlines to reduce sail.

"Come below, Uncle Thomas," urged Lucien. "It does no good to stay up here. You must try to get some rest."

Another wave crashed into the hull, sending a shudder through the oak timbers and rattling the brass six-pounders in their casings. The Duke shook the water from his sodden coat and reluctantly followed his nephew down the narrow hatchway and into the officers' wardroom. The two of them hunched forward to keep from knocking their heads in the cramped space as a young midshipmen materialized to take their wet outer garments away. The first lieutenant stumbled in right on their heels.

"Your pardon, Your Grace," he said. "The captain sends word that he will remain on deck until midnight watch, but he begs you to make use of his cabin for the remainder of the voyage."

"And how long will that be?"

The man began to scratch at his chin, then remembered in whose presence he was. The speedy sloop and its crew were more used to carrying dispatches than important passengers. He straightened as best he could before replying.

"The barometer is dropping, Your Grace, so the wind should die down soon. Now, with the weather coming from the north, and the taffrail showing a speed of . . ."

The Duke fixed him with an impatient glare.

"Ah, I should think we will land around daybreak."

"Thank you," replied the Duke, in a tone that indicated nothing less than dismissal.

The man slunk off.

Turning to Lucien, his uncle pulled a face and started to make his way aft. "I suppose you are right. Since the Fates seem to be conspiring against us, let us see if we can at least manage to snatch some sleep in this cursed weather." Another lurch caused him to grab on to the edge of the table to keep his balance. "Damned ship is worse than a skittish hunter. God grand us speed to touch down on English soil as soon as possible."

He reached the door of the cabin and yanked it open. Lucien followed him into a space barely bigger than a stall at Roxbury Manor, thankful once again that he had felt no urge to make the Navy his career. He hauled himself into a hammock that had been hastily strung up in a corner of the cabin while the Duke wedged himself into the captain's berth. Both of them wore a pained expression, which only worsened each time the rough sea sent the ship on its ear.

After a while, the Duke gave up even a semblance of trying to sleep. He struggled back up to a sitting position and stared glumly at the small oil lamp rolling wildly on its gimbals.

"If only Caroline would learn to temper her penchant for taking risk," he murmured out loud, though he was speaking more to himself than to his nephew. "Heaven knows she has more courage and wits than most, but she seems driven at times to foolhardiness." He shook his head. "Would that I knew why."

Lucien heard every word, but he hesitated in replying. There were times, it seemed, when his uncle still considered him a child, with only a child's grasp of reality. How would the Duke react to hearing a truth that might strike him as rather hard? Another wave crashed into the side. Well, perhaps now was as good a time as any to test the waters, thought the Viscount with a grim smile.

"I believe I could tell you."

The Duke sat up straighter. "You can?"

Lucien took a deep breath, then plunged on. "I think Caro is under the impression that she is, well, a . . . disappointment to you."

The Duke's jaw dropped in astonishment. "Why, of all the absurd things! Surely she cannot think . . ."

"She isn't a male," said Lucien simply.

"For God's sake, what difference does that make?" he cried. "She is my child! I love her beyond anything."

"Have you told her that?"

"I, well, that is . . . she *must* know." A note of uncertainty had crept into his normally self-assured tone.

"Uncle Thomas," said Lucien quietly, "I think she needs to hear it. You can be demanding, sir—sometimes it is hard to know whether one has lived up to your high standards. And for her, the task is even more daunting. As a female with intelligence, she sometimes finds her role in Society very . . . confusing."

He looked shaken. "I . . . I hadn't realized I was so unfair."

"No, not unfair. I didn't mean that at all. You have made us better for it, but in Caro's case, she is harder on herself than you will ever be. For you see, only she can learn to forgive herself for not being the heir."

The timbers of the ship creaked and groaned and the beam of the lamp rocked wildly, one moment illuminating a part of the Duke's face, then next moment leaving it in complete darkness. Lucien could see only that his uncle's fingers were steepled under his chin, but he couldn't make out his expression. When finally the Duke spoke again it was barely above a whisper.

"You have been infinitely more perceptive than I, Lucien. How could I be so blind? I . . . thank you for the advice."

"You are welcome, sir."

Chapter Eight

Caroline pulled her jacket tighter to her chest as she stood in the chill shadows and waited for the Earl to return. It seemed like an age since he had entered the small tavern set on a quiet side street. Probably having a nice joint of mutton, she thought with a scowl as her stomach growled a reminder that her last meal had been some hours ago. She wiggled her toes in the damp boots and vowed that if he didn't appear by the count of fifty, she was going in after him. After all, she had a full purse. A shilling was a shilling. Surely no barman would care overly what the pitch of a customer's voice was.

The thought of food—hot food—was so appealing she was almost disappointed when Davenport emerged before she had reached thirty-five and sauntered over to where she was hidden.

"The coaching inn is not far at all—just at the top of the hill and turn right. We are to look for the sign of The Flying Dolphin," he reported, keeping his voice low, head drawn close to hers. "Though it appears there is nothing that leaves for London until early morning."

"You've been drinking!" she accused.

"Well, one has to pay for information, one way or another," he reasoned. "It would have looked odd had I not lingered for a tankard."

"No doubt you had a decent meal too," she grumbled. "You were in there long enough."

"Feeling peckish?"

She was about to let loose with an angry rejoinder when he slid something out of his pocket and into her hand. An eel pastry, still hot to the touch.

"Mmmm."

The rich crust crumbled at her first bite, and a bit of the juice spilled down her chin. Davenport smiled as his finger came up to wipe it away.

"I would have brought two had I known you had the appetite of a boy, as well as the clothing. I thought ladies merely picked at their food."

Caroline popped the last morsel into her mouth. "I suppose that's true," she said, her voice now a good deal more cheerful. "But I'm far from a proper lady, as you've reminded me on more than one occasion. It comes in useful at tim—" Her words broke off at the sight of four figures suddenly looming out of the darkness behind the Earl.

Davenport started to spin around just as two of them grabbed hold of his arms. A third forestalled any struggle by producing a long-barreled pistol from the fold of his coat and aiming dead at the Earl's heart.

"Well, well, Davenport," sneered a voice from behind the figure with the weapon. "I see your tastes still include young boys." The speaker was a thick, heavyset man of average height, who punctuated his words with the slow slap of a stout walking stick against his meaty palm. As he stalked up to the Earl, his face, once passably handsome, was shown in the pale moonlight to have sagged into a state of pasty corpulence. But even the rolls of flesh could not hide the glint of pure malice in the beady eyes.

"How fortuitous that Barkley recognized you in the tavern." As he spoke, he surveyed the Earl's tattered garments with a curl of his lips. "Slumming tonight? Or have you come down in the world? This ain't your usual haunt."

"Be off, boy," said Davenport quietly. "This is no concern of yours."

"Yes, be off. You'll have to find some other gentleman with perverse tastes to pay for using you in an unnatural way." The butt of his stick came down hard on the Earl's chest. "You shouldn't have reneged on your vowels, Charles. Especially with me. But now you shall pay. And with interest." He motioned towards one of the other darkened side streets. "Let's take his bleeding lordship somewhere where we won't be disturbed."

Davenport allowed himself a slight smile. "I am afraid you are venting your spleen on the wrong audience. I may be Davenport, but not the one you want—Charles has been dead these four months."

The man's smug expression dissolved into one of rage. "What do you take me for—a idiot, and blind in the bargain?" he cried. "Did you think I wouldn't recognize you without a bottle and a doxie in your hands and your breeches down around your knees? Let me tell you, I would recognize that phiz in hell. Dead, you say! You are going to wish you *were* dead when I finish with you, you lying, cheating whoreson. I intend to break every bone in your body. Now take him away!"

The two men holding the Earl shoved him forward and the other two followed, with barely a cursory look around to see if anyone had observed them. It hardly mattered. Disagreements with fists, knives or worse were not uncommon in a rough port. Nobody with any sense was going to interfere.

Caroline had fallen back even further into the shadows at the Earl's veiled warning. After that, no one took the slightest notice of her. She bit her lip in dismay as she watched them take the Earl away. There was precious little she could do against four large—and armed—men. There was nothing for it but to obey Davenport's command. Her purse was full and her means to London left in only a few hours. Nothing stood in her way. It wasn't her fault he had been unfortunate enough to stumble into such a coil. No doubt he would survive.

It was no concern of hers. Hadn't he said as much?

Her hands clenched once or twice at her sides, then she hurried off across the cobblestones, swiftly yet silently. But instead of turning up the hill towards The Flying Dolphin, she slid into the inky darkness that had enveloped the Earl.

A muffled thud was followed by a sharp exhalation of air. As Caroline's eyes adjusted to the dim shadows, she saw the punch had dropped Davenport to his knees. His arms were still held by two of his captors while the ringleader rubbed his knuckles and circled around to deliver a vicious kick to the kidneys. The force of it sent the Earl face-down onto the stones.

"Pick him up," ordered the man who had dealt the blow. He gave a harsh laugh. "That is just the beginning."

The Earl was wrenched to his feet, then the walking stick slashed hard into his ribs, doubling him over.

The man with the pistol took a step closer to the others. "Come on, Johnny, share the sport. He's taken enough blunt off of me that I shall enjoy darkening those pretty deadlights."

"Very well." Stick tapping his boot, the leader stepped aside.

The slur of their words made it evident that they were all well in their cups. The one with the gun carelessly laid it on the ground and flexed his fingers as if to ensure they were ready to inflict as much damage as possible.

"Let's start with the face now," he drawled. "Perhaps the lightskirts won't be quite so pleased to see him once we've rearranged his looks." He sauntered over and grabbed Davenport's chin, lifting it to make an easy target.

His fist came back.

"That's quite enough."

Four heads jerked around.

"Oh, bloody hell," muttered Davenport.

Caroline stepped forward, pistol held at arm's length. "Let him go."

"Why, it's the damn boy!" exclaimed one of the ones holding the Earl.

The man with the stick took a step towards her. "Give me the gun, you sodding urchin, before I knock your teeth out as well."

A distinct click echoed off the surrounding brick walls as Caroline cocked the weapon.

"I am accorded to be a very good shot," she said evenly.

"There are four of us. And only one bullet, you fool," he snarled, but he didn't come any closer.

"Quite. So which one of you wishes to be the martyr?" She shifted her aim to the one holding Davenport's left arm. "You?"

He dropped his hold and retreated backwards.

"How about you?"

The man gripping the Earl's right arm slunk away to join his friend.

Davenport staggered slightly but managed to stay on his feet.

"Are you all right?" she asked.

"What a damn fool question—I suppose I shall live, but one never knows when one is around you," he snapped. "What the devil are you doing here, anyway? I told you to be off."

"Oh, stubble it, my lord. You should be damn grateful I *am* here," she retorted. "In fact, you might try to sound a little grateful, rather than growling at me as usual. You have to admit, it's hardly fair to blame *this* little incident on me."

The four men had listened to the brief exchange with increasing disbelief.

"Why, it's . . . it's a chit!" sputtered the man with the stick.

"And no less able to send you to your Maker," she replied, with a very credible attempt at a snarl.

The man fell back, his ponderous jaw dropping onto his chest.

"Now, are you going to stand there all night, Julian, or can we be on our way?"

Davenport limped past her, muttering darkly under his breath.

She found she was rather relishing her role. "Any of you bastards try to follow us, you'll get a bellyful of lead for your troubles."

Davenport stopped in his tracks. "You are actually enjoying this, aren't you?" he said through gritted teeth.

Caroline grinned. "Actually it's rather novel to be able to scrape *you* out of the mud for a change."

With a last flourish of the pistol, she backed down the street until the men were lost in the darkness. Then she turned and slipped an arm around Davenport's waist.

Caroline lit the small lantern and surveyed what fell within the faint circle of light with a slight frown.

"At least the straw is plentiful and looks moderately fresh." She turned back to where the Earl stood slumped against the rough-hewn door. "I think you had best lie down right away, sir, and let me see to your injuries. One of the stalls is empty and should provide a bit more shelter."

As she spoke, she gathered a few extra armfuls of hay and piled them into a semblance of a bed. Davenport made his way slowly across the narrow stable and sank down upon it, stifling a grunt of pain. His breathing had begun to sound less labored but the tight line of his mouth indicated he was still in a great deal of discomfort. Caroline spied a bucket under a bench piled high with an assortment of farrier's tools. She filled it with water from a wooden barrel standing by the door, then carried it back and knelt beside the Earl. There was the sound of fabric ripping.

"Ah, well, another shirt ruined," she remarked with a quirk of her lips as she dipped a strip of linen in the cold water and started to gently dab at Davenport's face.

He made a sound as if he meant to protest.

"Stay still, my lord, and let me see to those cuts without squirming around like a stuck pig."

Davenport finally found his tongue. "Would that they *had* stuck me and been done with it. It is getting tiresome to be—" He bit off an oath as Caroline touched a raw scrape on his cheek.

"Sorry," she muttered as she twisted out the cloth and applied a compress to the swelling.

"You are getting very good at this."

She gave a short laugh. "If you don't have a care, sir, your bones will soon be a match for mine."

That drew a reluctant smile from him. "A pair, aren't we?" he agreed. "What in Hades ever made you follow those men? Surely you could see they were in no mood to be trifled with. You could have gotten yourself in more trouble than you can imagine—as you see, it took them little time to figure out you were not an ordinary street urchin."

"And *you* could have gotten yourself in a worse state. I am well aware what mood they were in—the mood for blood."

"But not yours, as you saw. You should have gone on the the inn and taken the first coach to London. I could have handled the situation very well myself."

She cocked an eyebrow. "Indeed? If I had been one of those gentlemen, I'm sure I would have been quaking in my boots. Besides, you told me the coach didn't leave until close to dawn."

"Well, it was a damn foolish thing to do. Will you never learn to be sensible?"

"Probably not." Her hands worked at cleaning the rest of the scrapes with a touch more vigor than necessary and she was rewarded by seeing him wince slightly. "Stop ringing a peal over my head," she continued. "You've pulled my irons out of the fire more than once on this journey, at considerable risk to your own person. I owed you."

Davenport's expression hardened. "I'm sorry you felt compelled to put yourself in danger," he said stiffly. "No doubt you—what are you doing?"

Caroline undid the last button of his shirt and opened it to expose his chest. With a sharp intake of breath she stared down at the reddening welt across the ribs, then her eyes, hot with anger, raised to meet his.

"The cur!" she exclaimed. "What a bloody coward to have struck you thus when you could not protect yourself." Her hand was already running gently over the bruise. It lingered against the tanned flesh. "Do you think anything is broken?"

Perhaps it was simply the flickering light playing tricks, but the Earl could have sworn he caught a glimmer of tears. The idea was ludicrous, he told himself. Mayhap he was move feverish than he thought.

"You had best start minding your language, young lady. It's becoming as colorful as a lad's," he answered quietly. "And no, it's just a bruise. Nothing to be upset about. I assure you I've experienced far worse knocks in my time. It will take a lot more than this for me to come a cropper."

Caroline had begun to shiver slightly. The air had become distinctly colder. No doubt that was the reason. It didn't escape Davenport's notice and he reached out and pulled her down beside him.

"Lord, I am a selfish oaf," he muttered. "You are freezing, and exhausted to boot, I'm sure. It has been a . . . trying day." His arm curled around her waist and drew her even closer. "It is you who must try to sleep."

She found herself snuggling against his shoulder with nary a hesitation. "I thought they were going to . . . hurt you terribly." Her hand was still on his bare chest. It feathered across the muscled planes and dark curls as it drew his shirt closed. "You mustn't catch a chill," she murmured.

"Stop worrying about me. I assure you, I am feeling quite warm."

Davenport turned on his side and pulled her tight to him, wrapping his arms so that they came to rest right under her breasts. The back of her fit snugly into the crook of his body, like the piece of a missing puzzle. He hadn't been lying. He was acutely aware of the heat emanating from her. She made a small sound, then shifted slightly. Her rounded buttocks grazed lightly against the front of his breeches.

It was the most fiercely erotic sensation he had ever felt. He gritted his teeth as a jolt of desire throbbed throughout his entire body. Good Lord, he had never wanted a woman as badly as he wanted her at that moment. It was not just physical need—the reasons were almost too complex, too overwhelming to frame with words. All he knew was that he wanted to comfort and protect her, and at the same time arouse her desire to the same fever pitch as his own. He wanted her to cry out his name with abandon. She had said it once.

Julian.

He wanted her to say it again and again. He wanted her to—he gave up trying to make rational sense of it and simply closed his eyes.

His hand stole inside her man's shirt. It slipped up under the light chemise she wore under the thick linen and cupped one of her firm, round breasts. She started, then lay utterly still. Ever so gently, his thumb began to stroke the tender skin, then the nipple itself. To his satisfaction, it hardened almost immediately and her response to him was dizzying. Of its own accord, his other hand joined in caressing her.

Caroline gave a low moan. Her hips began moving restlessly from side to side against him. The Earl sucked in his breath. If she kept that up for much longer, he thought, he would end up disgracing himself like the callowest of schoolboys.

"Yes, my sweet urchin, it can be pleasurable for a lady too," he whispered as he nibbled at the lobe of her ear.

She made an unintelligible answer.

He slowly undid the buttons of her breeches and traced a path down her soft skin to the downy curls between her thighs. His fingers brushed gently through them, then sought even greater intimacy.

She gave a low cry.

He nearly cried out himself at feeling her honeyed dampness. My God, he thought, she wanted him too, and was sweetly ready for him.

"Has your husband never touched you thus?" he demanded.

"N-n-no," she managed to gasp.

"The selfish lout. He should be horsewhipped," he said hoarsely as he pressed a kiss against her hair.

His own arousal was at a fever pitch. A part of him wanted to strip the breeches from her at that instant and take her with a swift, hard passion. They were both so very ready. They both wanted it badly. He began fumbling with the fastenings of his own breeches when a disquieting thought somehow beggared its way into his consciousness.

He was acting no better than Charles, about to tumble another man's wife in the straw of a barn. The thought of it in that light managed to bank the fires of his desire. Not like this, he decided. He wouldn't allow them to be carried away by the heat of the moment—to couple like two animals in a stall.

But it wasn't so very wrong, argued another, more defiant voice in his head. She was an experienced lady, knowing full well what she was consenting to. Why, they would be acting no differently than half the *ton*. It was accepted behavior, if not condoned, so why shouldn't they indulge their passion? Besides, it added, she deserved to know a touch of pleasure, for no doubt her husband was a brute in the marriage bed as well.

A ragged sigh escaped his lips. For a brief instant, he found himself wishing he had the morals of his brother, as well as his looks. It wasn't in him, however. Perhaps he was a romantic fool, but if they did embark on a liaison, it would be amid candlelight, silk and champagne.

Steely resolve cooled his wild urges, even as she stirred under again under his touch and murmured his name. With an agonizing reluctance, he gently withdrew his hand and then circled her waist with his arm, drawing her tight against him.

"Julian?" she whispered. "Why . . . "

"Though it may nigh well kill me, let us wait," he answered softly, brushing another kiss over her tangled curls. "When I make love to you it will not be in a pile of straw, my dear." He rolled so that he was above her, elbows resting on either side of her shoulders, their faces mere inches apart. "I intend to make it special, so that you might know that relations between a man and woman can be more pleasurable than you have ever imagined, given your past experiences."

She made a strange sound in her throat.

"And I intend that it will be soon," he added, his voice edged with desire.

She smiled tentatively, not knowing quite how to answer. Her own emotions were a whirl of confusion. "I . . . I suppose you are right," she said raggedly, though she wasn't sure whether she felt relieved or disappointed that he had stopped when he did. As she struggled to make sense of her thoughts, her fingers came up to trace the faint line of the scar on his cheek. "Your eyes are so changeable. Right now they are such a clear blue—the storm clouds seem to have been blown to sea."

He kissed her once more, long and thoroughly.

When she ventured to speak again he pressed a finger to her lips. With a sigh, she fell asleep in his arms.

Davenport awoke before dawn as the horse in the stall beside them gave a kick to the splintered wood. Rough straw prickled his neck, his clothes were stiff with salt and his chin itched with a night's stubble. And that was hardly the worst of it. There was barely a part of his anatomy that did not pain him in some fashion. His spirits, however, hadn't felt so light in ages as he glanced down at the face cradled on his chest—that is, until he remembered she was someone else's wife.

Caroline's eyes opened slowly, then she sat up with a start.

"Oh!" A furious blush spread over her at the sight of the Earl's open shirt and her own disheveled clothing. "Ah . . . I imagine we had better be off if we are to catch the first coach," she said with a rush of words, struggling to button her breeches and rise at the same time in order to cover her confusion.

His hand stopped her fumblings. "Nay," he said gently. "We have time. We needn't rush." He brushed a wisp of straw from her loosened hair. "Caroline, there is no need to feel embarrassed—or guilty. Your husband doesn't deserve any loyalty for what he has done to you."

Her eyes dropped to the ground.

"Look at me, urchin."

She still refused to meet his gaze. "Do you still care for him, then?" His voice had become rather brittle.

"I . . ."

His eyes took on the color of cold steel as he waited for her to go on.

"I don't . . ."

"Yes?"

"I don't . . . have a husband."

Davenport could only stare at her in mute astonishment. "What?" he finally managed to sputter.

"I'm sorry. I let you believe that because it seemed, well, easier at the time."

"You mean to say you are not married?" He said the words slowly and deliberately, as if drawing them out might help him comprehend their full import.

She shook her head.

"Not ever?"

She shook it again.

"Bloody hell!"

He was on his feet in a trice, almost shouting as he paced furiously within the narrow confines of their refuge. A glance down at his bare chest caused him to miss a step as he hurriedly did up his shirt and yanked his coat closed. The string of oaths that followed set her ears to ringing, despite what she had heard escape the lips of her cousin on numerous occasions.

Her face turned ashen. "I didn't realize you would be so angry with me. I am so very sorry. Obviously you are regretting—"

"Regret?" His voice dropped considerably, then his hand raked through his hair. "I didn't mean—damnation, had I known you had no experience with men I never would have . . ."

His initial anger had cooled and the words trailed off as a look of self-loathing flooded his eyes. Now he was simply appalled at the magnitude of his own sins. How could he explain to her? "Good Lord, I am no better than Charles, debauching an innocent," he mumbled to himself.

Caroline's head flew up. "No! How could you ever think such a thing? You are nothing like your brother. Why, you are the most . . . honorable man I have ever met. Of course, I have had it explained to me that there are gentlemen who will try to force themselves on a lady, but it was not like that at all. If there is fault to be laid, it is with me—I am truly sorry if I have led you astray by my actions. I . . . I don't know exactly what happened last night." She shook her head in confusion and once again had to let her eyes slide away from his. "Luc—my cousin says men are wont to do things they will regret later when in their cups. Mayhap it is the same for ladies. I vow, I shall never touch a drop of brandy again!"

That drew a short bark of laughter from the Earl, despite his jumbled emotions. Why was it his normal world seemed to tilt on a strange axis when in proximity to this maddening chit, he couldn't help but wonder. Why, she had had him off kilter ever since he had first picked her up out of the mud—that thought suddenly brought him back to their present predicament. His brows drew together.

"If you have no husband, then who in Hades is after you with such a vengeance?"

She swallowed hard. "I don't know."

"Stop playing games with me," he said in a low voice. "I won't have it anymore." His eyes were clouded with anger. "I think by now I should have earned more than your damn guineas—I should have earned your trust."

"I don't know," she repeated. But before he could explode with any further angry words, she took his hand and pressed it up against her jacket. "Truly I don't. But I know what he wants."

A slight lump shifted under his fingers, causing his expression to turn into one of puzzlement.

Caroline let out a long breath. "You asked me a while back whether I had made off with the family jewels. Well, what I have here is infinitely more valuable than that. The fate of a number of people, and perhaps a country, rests in the pages I carry hidden in this packet. I don't know who it is that is pursuing it, but I know he is no friend of England, and that he has killed already to get hands on these documents. And as we have seen, he won't hesitate for a moment to do so again." She began to fiddle with the frayed cuff of the jacket, her eyes falling away from his. "So perhaps now you understand my reluctance to trust . . . anyone."

"Let alone a drunken wastrel."

"It has been some time since I have thought of you as that, my lord," she replied in a near whisper.

His face remained impassive. "How did you come by the papers?"

There was only the slightest pause before she answered. "My father is . . . involved with the government from time to time. These papers came by special courier to our home, but he had just left on a mission to the Continent."

"Why didn't the man take them on to London, then?" asked Davenport, though it took little imagination to figure out what had happened. Her next words, therefore, came as little surprise.

"He died on our doorstep."

The Earl shook his head. He could not suppress the scowl on his face or the edge of anger to his voice. "And your people allowed you to undertake the task of delivering the papers to London by yourself?"

Her chin came up. "They had little say in the matter."

"That I can well believe," he muttered through gritted teeth.

"Surely you wouldn't expect that I would ask a groom or a footman to risk his life. And Darwin, who has been with my family for ages, is well past his prime, though I should never say so to his face. It was my responsibility."

"Was there no male of your family? What of that damned—that cousin of yours?"

"There was no one but me." She struggled to control the slight quiver of her lips as memories of the past days flooded over her. "I daresay I have done as well as Luc—as he could have," she added stoutly. "Well, nearly as well. I doubt he would have allowed himself to be nipped in the alleyway."

"I daresay you have."

Davenport reached out, taking her by the elbow and drawing her down to sit beside him on the straw. Her arm remained in his grip, but his touch had become almost gentle. He cleared his throat while pondering how to proceed, then spoke again.

"Tell me what happened."

She did.

He said nothing during her recounting of the stormy night, the mad flight and the terrible crash, though the increasing tension in his body gave hint as to his feelings. Caroline finished her story with a slight exclamation that caused the Earl to start.

"Sir, if you do not loosen your hold on me, I fear I shall have another blotch of purple to add to my formidable collection."

His fingers flew open, but remained resting lightly on her sleeve. "You still haven't told me who you are."

She started to speak, then stopped. The silence yawed between them, the only answer it seemed he would receive. A look of hurt passed over his features, quickly replaced by no expression at all.

"Quite right," he said, an edge to his voice. "No need for

the hired lackey to know anything more." Before she could protest, he scrambled to his feet. "Where did you put the pistol from last night?"

She pointed to where it lay in the dirt.

He picked it up and carefully inspected the priming. "Come on then, let's be off," he snapped as he slid the weapon into his coat pocket. "There is even more reason to get you to London without further delay. At least now it seems likely that I shall actually get my money."

Since his back was deliberately turned towards her, there was no way he could see the stricken look on Caroline's face.

Chapter Nine

The sails backed, the helmsman shifted course a few degrees and the ship ghosted into the crowded harbor. At the first lieutenant's crisp command, chains rattled and the anchor plunged into the murky depths. Although the moon still cast a faint glow over the water, the Duke and his nephew were aboveboard and pacing the deck before the last sail was furled.

The captain approached, the set of his shoulders betraying a hint of nerves. It wasn't every day that his small vessel was commandeered by a peer of the realm—and one in such a dire haste to reach his destination. He swallowed as he considered that the storm had possibly sunk all hopes of advancement.

"Your Grave," he said stoutly. "I regret that I could not deliver you here sooner . . ."

His apology was gruffly interrupted. "You have my thanks, Captain. You've done well, sir. The admiralty shall hear of it."

The officer's anxiety dissolved into elation. Perhaps it was not merely a flight of fancy to imagine being made post captain—he caught himself and put aside such dreams until later as he caught the last of the Duke's words.

". . . ashore immediately."

Fortunately, he had expected no less. A longboat was already being lowered, eight muscled sailors ready to take the oars. The ladder was lowered and with a minimum of cere-

mony—no pipes, no officers lined in salute—the two passengers were helped down the steep, pitching side into the
small craft. It fairly flew towards shore, propelled by
bosun's stentorious command and the promise of an extra
ration of rum for all hands on making land in record time.

The Duke breathed a sigh of relief on setting foot on
English soil. He took Lucien's arm and hurried awkwardly
across the dock, legs still rolling with the gait of the sea.

"Not much longer now," he muttered as his eyes swept
the cobbled streets.

The sky was just beginning to lighten with glow of dawn
and the wharves were nearly deserted, save for a few drays
unloading coils of hemp and barrels of tar in front of a row
of warehouses. The Duke grabbed at the closest driver and
barked a demand to be taken to the coaching inn. The man
regarded the elegant figure as if he had just emerged from
Bedlam until he heard the heavy chink of the purse thrust
under his nose. With a grunt, he heaved the last of his load
onto the street and motioned for the two figures to climb
into the back of his vehicle. The crack of a whip sprung the
draft horses, whose pace amounted to little more than a
plodding trot. Still, it was not too long before they arrived
at their destination.

The smell of coffee seemed ambrosial to Lucien as he
slid into a chair and took a sip of the steaming brew. The
main room of the inn was already filling with people despite the early hour. Several men, gentlemen by their looks,
conversed together in low murmurs at a table in the corner
while a fat farmer and his wife next to them put the last
knots in several bulging sacks. An elderly curate was already nursing a tankard of ale while other passengers for
the mail coach simply sat in sleepy silence, eyes not venturing up from the ill-swept floor.

Outside, the ostlers were hitching a fresh team to a sleek
phaeton painted a garish black and yellow, all the while

coming under a steady stream of invectives from a fop-
pishly dressed young man. Lucien watched the argument
escalate as he took another sip. Finally, the gentleman
seemed resigned that his heated words were having no effect on the men save to elicit a veiled sneer or two. With a
hitch of his caped driving coat, he mounted his vehicle with
as much dignity as possible and cracked the whip.

The young Viscount was not the only spectator to the
scene. From the corner of his eye, he noticed two men
standing by the far end of the stables. They were rather disheveled, their hats pulled down low, collars turned up
against the bite of the morning air. The taller one bent to
converse with his companion, then drew him back farther
into the shadows. Lucien shrugged as he turned his attention back to his coffee. Laborers heading to London for
work, he thought. Or two seamen tired of a brutally harsh
life. In any case, it was no concern of his.

The Duke sat down beside his nephew and took the pro-
ferred cup, a look of grim satisfaction on his weathered
face. "It took a little persuasion, but we have two carriages,
with two teams of decent horses."

Lucien smiled faintly as he wondered how many guineas
had changed hands and how many disgruntled people
would be cooling their heels until later. Not that the cost
mattered. Not that anything mattered, save for finding Caroline.

"I shall go directly to London," continued his uncle.
"You are to drive with all speed to Roxbury Manor. Let us
hope between the two of us, we shall find her . . . un-
harmed."

A sharp blast of a horn announced the arrival of the mail
coach bound for London. A number of people rose and hurried into the courtyard, knowing full well that any dawdling
would result in being left behind. The Duke paid no little
heed to the commotion. "Best finish your coffee quickly,"

he advised. "As soon as the mail has departed, the ostlers will have us off in a trice."

Lucien set down his cup and both men scraped their chairs back, taking no note of the two slightly disreputable figures that climbed aboard the mud-splattered coach along with the rest of the passengers.

Davenport muttered a curse under his breath. "I had engaged a private conveyance and a fast team, then the damn fellow suddenly informed me that an important personage had precedence over my request." He pulled a face. "Unfortunately, neither my person nor my purse could argue with him. We have no choice but the mail coach."

Caroline avoided looking at him. "I'm sure it will make little difference, my lord. And perhaps it is even better this way. I should imagine the chances of being noticed are slimmer if we remain in a crowd."

He merely grunted, but she noticed that his hand rarely left the pocket containing the pistol. The Earl was certainly keeping his guard up, she thought glumly, and not leastways against her. As the heavy coach rumbled into the courtyard, he urged her forward.

"For God's sake, keep your hat pulled down and pray, don't utter even a word during the trip," he whispered as they pushed towards the cluster of people waiting to squeeze into the dark interior.

There was little danger of that. It seemed they had had precious little to say to each other since leaving the shelter of the stable.

She found herself wedged in between a country squire reeking heavily of scent and a merchant clutching a small parcel to his chest, as if he feared highwaymen would accost them at any moment. The Earl took a seat directly opposite her, promptly dropped his head to his chest and began to snore.

   Caroline lowered her eyes to the grimy floorboards, for she feared sleep would be nigh impossible.

   Drat the man!

   Did he have windmills in his head? How could he imagine she didn't trust him, or thought of him as some sort of lackey? That wasn't it at all. As she reflected on what, exactly, had kept her silent, honesty compelled her to admit it was fear. She had come to value the feisty camaraderie that had developed between them, with none of the artificial constraints of Society coloring their actions—why, she even found she liked his curses and his irritable moods. She liked it that he passed her a bottle of brandy, that he told her she looked a fright. He treated her like a real person, not some porcelain doll devoid of brains or bottom. All because he thought her a lady of no consequence.

   She was loath to give it up. Only Lucien had ever treated her like that, but this was different. How, she could not explain, even to herself. But once he knew the truth of who she was, that bond was likely to prove as chimerical as the lightness in his eyes. Of course he would find out soon enough, but, like a child clinging to the last shreds of a cherished blanket, she would cling to what they had as long as she could.

   There was another matter, too. She swallowed hard as a different sort of fear crept up upon her consciousness. She had learned he was a man of honor. What if he felt compelled to offer for her when he learned her rank? There could be no question as to whether their intimacies had thoroughly compromised her. Especially after . . . last night. The very thought of what had taken place brought on a rush of color and she needed no admonition from the Earl to keep her face buried in the folds of her jacket.

   Ruined.

   Funny, but she did not feel ruined in the least. Or sorry.

   In her mind there was nothing shameful in what had happened—the blush rose more from the realization that, in fact, she wanted very much for him to carry out his promise to take her to bed. Perhaps her cousin was right in pronouncing her a hopeless hoyden. She had always rebelled against the rules, and this was no exception, though again, she could not begin to put into words why her actions were not beyond the pale. It certainly wasn't that she was no better than she should be. Never had she dreamed of allowing a gentleman such liberties with her person, but things had happened in such a way that it was almost as if with his intimacies, the Earl had been giving a part of himself rather than taking something from her.

But what was the Earl thinking?

He had been undeniably angry on learning she was an innocent. Thankfully, discussion along those lines had been deflected by the concerns of their current situation but she had no allusions that the matter had been laid to rest. The flicker of emotion in his eyes told her that, more eloquently than any words. If she were a mere nobody, it might be easier to convince him he had no obligation. As a Duke's daughter, the matter was infinitely more complicated.

Suddenly, her throat tightened. Did he think her truly sunk in the mud for allowing his caresses? Or worse, had he taken a disgust to her? Perhaps his haunted look had stemmed from the fact that he felt hopelessly trapped between his sense of honor and the thought of being leg-shackled to such a wanton and willful wife for the rest of his life. After all, he had made no secret as to his opinion of her behavior.

No, she was hardly the sort of lady a gentleman—even one with the sort of reputation as the Earl of Davenport— would wish to offer for.

Her eyes closed, more to cover the sting of tears than with any real hope that sleep would bring a welcome respite from such disquieting thoughts.

*   *   *

"Open your peepers, lad." A boot jostled against hers. "Let us climb down and stretch our legs while they change the horses."

Had she really nodded off?

Davenport jerked his head towards the door, impatient to quit the closeness of the crowded coach. Still groggy with sleep, Caroline hauled herself up and stumbled down the steps. Had it not been for the Earl's steadying hand, her wobbly legs might have failed to keep her upright.

"Are you all right?" he asked in a low voice as he guided her to the far end of the yard. "You look bloody awful."

She turned to regard the tangled locks straggling out from beneath his misshapen hat, the unshaven cheeks, one of which was beginning to take on a mottled purpling under the scruff, and the general state of disarray of the rest of his shabby clothes.

"You are not exactly looking like a pink of the *ton* yourself," she snapped. "As to the question of whether I am all right, given the fact that I haven't had a decent meal in Lord knows when—not to speak of clean sheets or a bath—and that I am traveling with someone who would as soon bite my head off at every turn than not, I am no worse than should be expected."

Davenport let his grasp fall away. He had the grace to look slightly discomfited as he dropped his gaze to the muddy tips of his boots. "If you will wait here, I will see if I can scrape up something decent to eat inside, though the odds look grim."

He returned with a wedge of dry cheddar, a crust of bread and an apple whose skin was as shrivelled as an old granny's. Caroline's eyes flew past the meager offerings to drink in the steaming mug of tea he held cradled against his chest. Without a word, he passed it to her. She let the heat seep into her chilled, chafed hands for a moment before raising it to her lips.

"Is it that bad?" he asked abruptly.

She stopped in mid-swallow, confused. "What?"

"My, er, disposition. Do I cut up at you as terribly as you say?"

She pressed the mug up to her cheek, still reveling it its comforting warmth. "Oh, that. I don't mind," she said softly. "I've gotten rather used to it."

A muscle in his jaw twitched and he looked as if to say something else when the rush of people elbowing their way back into the coach indicated that it was nearly ready to leave. The Earl jammed his hands into his pockets and kicked at an errant pebble.

"We'd better make haste," he muttered. "It wouldn't do to be left behind at this stage."

The ostlers were already buckling the last bits of harness, and as they hurried towards the waiting vehicle to regain their places, neither of them noticed a lone rider set off at a gallop towards London.

Davenport restrained the urge to reach out and tuck an errant lock of hair back under the ridiculous man's cap that obscured most of her face. Enough of it was visible to show that the guarded expression she had worn since morning had softened in repose, only the heightening the look of vulnerability she took such pains to hide. His chest constricted slightly, unrelated to the bruising of his ribs. At least she was able to sleep, he thought, in spite of the horrors she had been through.

It was more than *he* could manage, despite the feigned snores. Her revelations had him in such a state that he didn't know whether to shake her until her teeth rattled or cover that expressive mouth with another kiss until she cried out his name with the same passion as she had last night. A harried smile stole to his lips—for then again, hadn't she been knocking his world akilter ever since that first morning when she opened her eyes and promptly planted him a facer? He nearly laughed aloud at the memory, then sobered considerably in the next moment.

It was no laughing matter. An unaccustomed heat crept over his face as he recalled his actions of last night. Good Lord, he was truly no better than his brother. No doubt she had been exhausted. No doubt she had been in a state of shock. No doubt she had been, well, tipsy! He had taken advantage of her, no matter that she had not . . . sought to discourage his advances. The flush deepened as he thought about his hand roving inside her breeches. Whatever had possessed him to lose himself so utterly to the heat of the moment? He had had his share of affairs and mistresses, but always within the boundaries of his own carefully constructed rules. Well, last night they had proved as effective as a sand fortress against the incoming tide. His vow to remain in strict control of his emotions had been swept away as easily as a speck on the strand. What he had experienced in the past was desire, physical need. What he had experienced last night was passion—and a need of some other sort.

It shook him to the very marrow.

His eyes pressed tightly closed. Here he had vowed to stay free of emotional entanglements and devote his energies to his estate and what had happened, weak fool that he was? She was not a raving beauty. Neither was she a pattern card for demure behavior or fragile femininity. She was, in short, all that a lady should *not* be.

The chit was vocal with her opinions, she rode astride, she used decidedly unladylike language, she didn't swoon at the first hint of unpleasantness. And to make matters worse, she was long and willowy when he usually preferred tiny and rounded.

So what was it? The Earl nearly gave a bark of ironic laughter, at the same time repressing an urge to tug his hair out by the roots. What was it? he repeated to himself. Very simple—she was vocal with her opinions, she rode astride, she used decidedly unladylike language, she didn't swoon at the first hint of unpleasantness. And furthermore, she didn't blink at his curses and only grinned at his irritable set-downs.

She tolerated his fits of ill temper and had risked her own life to save his skin. Had he left anything out? he demanded as his teeth gritted together. Oh, and she never used tears to twist a man to her own desires.

She was brave. She was loyal. She had pluck to the bone, and a sense of humor. She—who the devil was she?

If he had felt rather queasy before, the thought of that question made him positively ill. He was not a total gudgeon. Highly sensitive dispatches, couriers to a private estate—it took little imagination to figure out her father was a very important man.

But why the devil wouldn't she tell him who?

There were any number of possible explanations but one sprang foremost to mind. She wanted to walk away from him at the end of this, hoping that what had passed between them would remain as unknown as her real identity. The import of her silence was as clear as any words she might have uttered. She wanted nothing to do with the Earl of Davenport, especially now that he had shown his true character, one not so very different from that of his infamous twin.

No doubt that accounted for the fact that she could barely force herself to look at him since morning.

An opportunistic rake. And an ill-mannered, bearish one at that—at least Charles had had a modicum of charm to sweeten the bitter aftertaste of his actions. Is that how she thought of him? Was she frightened? Ashamed? Or merely willing herself to block out the feel of his bare chest, the touch of his fingers as she would the rest of her nightmarish experience? She was strong enough to forget and go with her life as if they had never met.

But was he?

Another question arose. He wondered whether she fully realized that her reputation was in his hands. She might be willing to put what had happened out of her mind, but one word from him, dropped discreetly among the *ton*, would ruin her forever, regardless of who her father was. Or would she consider the thousand pounds a payment for his silence as well? The growl that rumbled in his throat caused the two men seated on either side of him to edge away in apprehension.

And he thought he had problems when only confronted by merciless creditors, a bankrupt estate and a disgraced name.

The gentleman crumpled the note and tossed it into the fire, allowing himself a small smile of satisfaction. His coachman had finally redeemed himself somewhat from the botch he had made of things.

So. She was nearly here. It was time to put his plan into action—one that would not fail.

A short while later a hackney pulled up in front of an elegant town house on Grosvenor Square. The occupant was dressed for the occasion in modest attire, as befitted his station. He carefully smoothed his hair and straightened his simply tied cravat before assuming an expression of grave concern and stepping forth from the vehicle. He rapped with a touch of urgency upon the heavy oak door. The butler answered almost immediately. His craggy features softened somewhat at the sight of a familiar face.

"Please come in, sir. I shall inform his lordship that you wish to speak to him." The last was phrased as a question.

"If you please, Jenkins," he answered politely. "That matter is rather important, I fear, else I wouldn't have disturbed him during the hours of his work."

The butler nodded sagely. "If you will wait in the—"

"Of course. I shall find my own way."

Jenkins understood the implied urgency and hurried off.

A bit later, a tall gentleman, height minimized by shoulders stooped from years of hunching over books, entered the room. His spectacles were pushed up to nest in a thatch of unruly grey locks and his face wore a vague air of consternation at being pulled from his inner sanctum.

"You wished to see *me*, Mr. Farrington?" he said, his tone implying his opinion of what such a meeting was likely to yield. "Jenkins has said as much, of course, but I don't understand . . ."

No, of course you don't, you doddering sapskull, thought Farrington to himself, all the while keeping the solicitous smile pasted on his face. But when he spoke, his words echoed the same false emotions as his expression.

"Indeed, I do," he interrupted smoothly. "It is a matter of great importance, sir." He withdrew a folded paper from his immaculate serge coat and waved it under the older man's nose. "I have just now received a special dispatch from His Grace." If the old fool thought to question it, he had no qualms that the handwriting would pass muster, even under the scrutiny of the Duke's own brother. After all, hadn't he been handling the man's correspondence for the past four years and more?

But Sir Henry made no move to inspect the document. At the mention of the Duke, his face became troubled. "Has . . . has something happened to Thomas or Lucien?" he stammered.

"No," assured Farrington. "It concerns Lady Caroline."

"But my niece is safe at Rox—"

"Quite. And the Duke wishes her to remain so. It has come to his attention that she may be in grave danger—"

He paused for effect, letting the other man absorb the full import of what he had just said. The charade was working to perfection—Sir Henry's expression had changed from one of concern to one of outrage. Just as he made as if to speak, Farrington cut him off and continued his prepared speech.

"He writes that he depends on you, sir, protect her from harm."

"Of course!" cried Sir Henry. "I may not be as adventurous as Thomas, but the devil take me if I would allow anyone to threaten Caroline!"

Farrington smiled primly. "His Grace has every confidence in you."

"What does he wish me to do?"

"He wants you to leave at once for Roxbury Manor. With timely warning, and you to oversee the household, disaster may be averted."

"Jenkins!" roared Sir Henry.

The butler appeared quickly enough that it seemed likely his ear had been glued to the keyhole.

"Have the traveling carriage brought around immediately!"

Farrington suppressed a smug laugh. "Sir, His Grace also suggests that you take Jenkins with you, as well as your footmen. It cannot hurt to be fully prepared."

Jenkins thrust out his chest and drew himself up to full height. "I shall be honored to help the family in any way."

Sir Henry chewed on his lower lip, "But that will mean leaving the house without a man to watch over it. What if . . ."

The critical moment had arrived. With a slight clearing of his throat Farrington spoke up again. "Sir, if I may be so bold, I would be happy to offer my services here in order to be of help to His Grace."

The other man clapped him on the shoulder. "No wonder Thomas thinks so highly of you, Mr. Farrington. You are sure you do not mind? It may be . . . dangerous."

"I don't mind." Farrington made a little bow in order to hide his smirk of triumph. "I don't mind at all."

The mail coach lurched to a stop at the busy posting inn on the outskirts of London. It was nearly dark yet the yard was filled with the stomping of hooves, the creaking of harnesses and the muttered curses of the ostlers as they sought to make the change as quickly as possible and get the various phaetons, curricles and coaches on their way.

Caroline and the Earl dismounted, stiff with travel and unspoken concerns. She hesitated at the entrance of the bustling establishment. Since setting out from her father's estate, nothing had seemed important save reaching the city with the documents from France. Yet now that she had arrived safe and sound, she was strangely reluctant to acknowledge that the journey—and all that had taken place—was over and done with. Davenport gave her little time to stew about it, however. As usual, he took her arm none too gently and moved her from blocking the doorway.

"Wait here," he said gruffly. "I'll see to arranging for you to be taken to—wherever you are going." A scowl darkened his already stormy countenance as he seemed to chew on the words. "And try to stay out of trouble, for once."

Odious man, she thought. As if she had meant to cause any of the problems that had befallen them.

He returned in a few minutes. "We are in luck. There are a few hackneys returning to the City after discharging their passengers. One shall come by directly." He stopped to clear his throat, and when he continued, his voice sounded strangely pinched. "I . . . Do you wish that I accompany you to your destination?"

Caroline failed to meet his eyes. "I don't think that is necessary, sir. I believe we are well out of danger now."

Only the tightening of his jaw betrayed any emotion on

his part. "Very well," he said curtly. "I shall need to ask you for some of the blunt for my own ride."

She removed a few coins and handed him the rest of the purse.

"Where . . . will you go?"

Davenport seemed to weigh his options as he stared at the bulging leather bag in his palm. Then, with a slight curl of his lips, he tucked it into his pocket.

"It is of no matter to you," he answered harshly. "You know where to deliver the rest. And don't forget you owe me for the horse as well." He sucked in his breath. "There's no charge for the . . . extra service, though I know of plenty of females who get paid handsomely for such things."

Caroline recoiled as if struck. Her face drained of all color.

The hackney arrived and he turned on his heel and stalked off, not waiting to see her off. She climbed blindly into the musty interior, hoping no one had remarked on the odd sight of a lad with tears streaming down his face.

Davenport rounded the corner of the inn and quickly slipped into another hackney after barking a set of terse orders at the driver. A slap of the reins set the vehicle in motion, throwing the Earl back up against the worn squabs. Pain shot through his ribs, but it was nothing compared to the mental lashing he was doling out to himself.

What in the name of Hades had possessed him to say such a monstrous thing? She might have cut him to the quick with her obvious desire to have him well out of her life, but it had not been a deliberate cruelty.

His hand raked through his hair. He had meant to hurt her. Yet seeing her face twist in shock had only made him feel even more miserable. Rather than proving that he had regained mastery over his emotions, it mocked the fact that his vaunted self-control had somehow slipped away, leaving him raw, vulnerable.

He felt defenseless, and it frightened him more than he cared to admit.

A bitter smile twitched at his lips. Well, he had learned to protect himself from other slings and arrows in life. Surely he would learn to block this out as well.

For if he admitted to himself that he cared for her, he was utterly lost.

The horses slowed and the ruts gave way to smooth cobblestones. Davenport glanced out the grimy window and saw they were approaching the fashionable area of Mayfair, with its well-lit streets and imposing dwellings. Up ahead was the dark shape of another lumbering vehicle. True to his orders, the driver had kept right on the tail of the hackney carrying Caroline. The Earl sank back in his seat, satisfied. In light of his recent behavior, she had every reason to think him a cad, but he had made a promise and he meant to keep it. He would see her safely to her destination, regardless of whether she wanted him to or not.

He would damn well earn every farthing of that thousand pounds.

Caroline bounded up the polished marble steps and let the knocker fall in a series of impatient raps. It seemed an age before the door cracked open and a pair of dark eyes peered out into the night.

"Be off, urchin."

Caroline had all but forgotten about the rather disreputable figure she must be presenting. She hastily shoved her worn boot into the gap to keep the door from being slammed in her face.

"Where is Jenkins?" she demanded. "And who the devil—oh, is it you, Mr. Farrington? Forgive my rather unorthodox appearance, but I shall explain everything shortly."

Her father's secretary fell back a step or two. "Lady Caroline?" he gasped, his hand flying up to his chest in surprise.

"Sorry to give you such a shock." She stepped into the entrance hall and tore off her cap. "Where are all the servants? And Uncle Henry?" she asked as she removed the pins and shook out her hair.

"Why, they have left for Roxbury Manor not an hour ago in response to an urgent letter from your father."

Caroline's lips compressed. "They will have a long journey for naught."

Farrington's eyes were still widened in amazement. They now slowly traveled up from her ragged breeches to her streaked face. "Are . . . are you all right?" he ventured.

She let out a sigh. "It is a long story, but yes."

Now that she was finally here, within the solid walls of her own home, surrounded by the reassuring presence of familiar things, she felt an overwhelming weariness steal over her. For an instant, her knees buckled slightly.

A hand steadied her shoulder and the sound of Farrington's voice, dripping with concern, oozed through the fogginess clouding her brain.

"Lady Caroline, let me help you to a chair."

"No, I'll be fine." Her eyes pressed closed. She didn't dare sit down, not yet. "If you would ring for a maid, I'll go directly upstairs." She envisioned a tub, filled to the brim with steaming suds, and a soft bed with clean sheets.

His hand remained where it was. "Your father mentioned something else." He cleared his throat. "Have you got . . . the papers?"

She hesitated for a moment, a frown clouding her face, then her expression lightened.

"Yes, of course you would know about that. Well, never fear. I have them safe." As she spoke, she patted at the breast of her jacket.

A gleam of pure malice flashed in his eyes before the lids dropped to mask his emotion. He lowered his voice as well, to a conspiratorial whisper. "I can only imagine what you have endured to reach London—your father naturally confided in me that there exists a traitor in our midst. Why don't you let me relieve you of the burden? I shall see they are delivered into the right hands, I assure you."

Caroline shook her head. "How very kind of you, but I have carried them this far, and I shall keep them until I can turn them over to my father."

His fingers unconsciously dug into her skin.

"Mr. Farrington, I think you may release me." She tried to keep her tone light to avoid causing him any embarrassment. "I promise that my collapse is not imminent."

All at once he was shaking her. "Give them to me!"

Caroline tried to pull away. "Mr. Farrington!"

He kept hold of her jacket and nearly wrenched her off her feet. "You damn bitch. You've caused me more than enough trouble—but no more. Now give me those documents!"

"My God. You!" She stared at him, unbelieving. "But why?"

"Why?" he repeated. "Are you daft? Do you think I plan to live the rest of my life accepting my station as an ill-paid younger son, having to bow and scrape in front of dolts like your father, who have had the damn luck of birth rather than brains, like me? I think not! Unfortunately I shall have to leave a tad sooner than I had planned, but my last delivery will set me up quite nicely—I shall live very well on the Continent."

She tried to twist out of his grasp as she let out a loud cry for help.

"Go ahead and yell all you wish," he sneered. "There is no one to hear you. I've sent the rest of the servants to their quarters. And don't expect that rakehell Davenport this time around. If he's not lying foxed in some gaming hell, he's lying with his manhood up some lightskirt, now that he's finished with you." His face took on an ugly leer. "Always prancing around in front of me, with your hoydenish ways, I always knew you were no better than you should be. Gave the Earl a good ride, did you? Perhaps I'll see for myself before I leave."

Her fist caught him smack on the nose.

Farrington let out a scream of rage as blood spurted onto his snowy shirtfront.

"You bitch!" he roared again as he struck her hard across the temple.

Dazed, Caroline would have fallen to the floor if he hadn't had such a tight hold of her jacket. As she hung limply in his grasp, his free hand pawed the inside of the garment, ripping at its lining. With a grunt of triumph, he came away with the oilskin packet.

It was her turn to feel a wave of fury. The sight of the precious papers, those she had fought so hard to keep safe, now in the possession of the enemy after all gave her new strength to fight back. Rather than struggling to break free, she launched herself right at him, her nails raking down his cheeks. Both of them stumbled backwards, colliding with an ornate mahogany case clock set near the curved staircase. A corner of it caught Caroline's brow, knocking her farther off balance. It gave Farrington just the time he needed to recover and knock her to the floor with another ringing blow. He stood over her, a harsh laugh escaping from him as he drew a small dagger from the depths of his pocket.

"Step away from the lady, lest you want your guts spilling onto your shirt as well."

The click of the pistol being cocked put an exclamation point to Davenport's words.

Caroline managed to raise her head a few inches off the Aubusson carpet. "Still having to scrape me out of the mud, I'm afraid," she croaked before falling into a dead faint.

Chapter Ten

Davenport took another step into the entrance hall and slowly closed the door.

"Lay the documents on the side table, then step away from Lady Caroline."

Farrington hesitated, his eyes narrowing, then darting from the floor to all of the possible egresses from the hall-way.

A grim smile came to the Earl's lips. "Go ahead. I should welcome an excuse to pull the trigger, for unfortunately, my honor as a gentleman prevents me from shooting even such a cowardly cur as you down like a savage dog, though it is all you deserve."

The other man ground his teeth, then reluctantly tossed the packet onto the polished wood. With a murderous look in his eye, he fell back a few paces from Caroline's prostrate form.

Davenport then moved deliberately to the side table, all the while never taking his eyes from the Duke's traitorous secretary. He took up the slim oilskin square and tucked it carefully into the bosom of his shirt. With another few strides, he was at Caroline's side, crouching and gently raising her head and shoulders with one arm. The pistol, however, never wavered in its aim at the other man's chest.

"A charming pair," sneered Farrington. "The *ton* shall no doubt find the acquaintance a, shall we say, fascinating topic for conversation. But now, let us be done with the

touching charade. How much do you want?" His face relaxed slightly as he began to feel himself on familiar
ground. "I imagine you are here since it suddenly occurred
to you that the possibilities for blackmail are rather limit-
less. How much has she paid you already? I assure you, I
am in a position to offer you more—much more." His hand
made a suggestive gesture towards his pocket. "Think on it
—you will have plenty of money right away, with none of
the wait or the tedium of extracting regular payments. Decide quickly, however." The calculating smile that finished
off his words left little doubt as to what he imagined the response would be. His hand was already reaching for the
bulging purse in his coat.

A muscle twitched in the Earl's face as he made no effort
to hide his contempt.

"On second thought, perhaps you have given me more
than ample reason for ridding the world of your scurvy
presence."

Farrington blinked, uncomprehending. A slight sheen of
sweat began to form at his temples. Cunning and guile had
seen him through any number of desperate situations—and
of course, money. Words and force might fail at times, but
the chink of gold upon gold? Never.

Was he dealing with a madman?

His brow furrowed and he essayed another tack. "Ah, a
canny bargainer, I see. You impress me, sir. Your reputation
would not lead one to think you so clever." There was an
exaggerated pause to let the compliment sink in. "I admit it,
you hold the upper hand. What else do you want?"

Davenport merely stared at him.

"Come, man! Name your price!" There was a note of rising panic in Farrington's voice, as well as disbelief.

Still no answer, just lips curled in loathing. When finally
the Earl did speak, it was a low, gentle murmur, too soft for
any ears but Caroline's to comprehend, as he sought to

bring her around. Though his words were for her only, his eyes still remained riveted on the man in front of him.

Farrington had by now worked himself into a veritable rage. To Davenport it seemed that never had a face more resembled an image of the devil incarnate. The other man raised his hands in a menacing gesture and took a convulsive step towards the Earl.

A gesture with the pistol caused him to reconsider. But even standing still, he remained quivering with impotent fury.

Davenport found himself wondering whether the man's next move would be cause to pull the trigger, and whether he would truly feel as little compunction at ending a human life, however flawed, as he did now. The answer would remain a mystery, as the front door suddenly flung open.

Farrington's arms, still raised, flew out wider. "Your Grace!" he cried, with little need to feign a tone of fervent relief. "Thank God you have come! We are saved!"

Indeed, the Duke of Cheviot had entered his house, caped greatcoat flung back from his imposing form to allow full aim for the brace of long-barreled pistols clutched in his hands. His thunderous look became even darker at taking in the scene in front of him.

The Duke's secretary hesitated not a whit in taking hold of the opportunity the Fates had so fortuitously dropped in his grasp. His finger pointed accusingly at the disheveled figure of the Earl.

"I tried to stop him, but I couldn't—he fought me off." Farrington touched at the ugly red marks scarring his cheeks for emphasis. "He attacked Lady Caroline, the cur, and was just now going to . . ." He contrived to falter quite convincingly, as if the thought of what might have happened to the young lady was too much to bear. "He took something from her jacket. It's hidden inside his shirt."

The Duke stalked over to the Earl. His boot lashed out, knocking the pistol from Davenport's unresisting hand.

"Put my daughter down, very slowly, then get up. If you have harmed—"

"She has taken a knock to the head, but her pulse is strong and her breathing is normal. I trust she will awaken with nought but a sore brow." He laid her gently down on the floor and stripped off his jacket to tuck under her head. Then he did as he was told, all the while trying to place the figure before him. The man looked vaguely familiar, but he couldn't recall the name. The rank, however, was clear. He shook his head slightly. The chit didn't do things by half, did she, he thought.

The Duke was barely able to contain his rage. "My God. I recognize you," he exclaimed as his mouth quirked in disgust. "A lord, no less. I know quite well what a worthless reprobate you are, but a traitor to your class and your country as well? I should throttle your worthless neck here and now." And he looked quite capable of carrying out the deed, if his hands hadn't been fully occupied.

Farrington began to sidle towards the door. "I shall fetch an armed guard and notify Whitehall of what is happening."

Davenport's expression remained unreadable. "I suggest you keep your secretary from disappearing, sir. When Lady Caroline recovers consciousness, you shall hear a very different tale from her lips. The traitor here is not I."

"Liar," spat Farrington. His eyes sought out the Duke. "Surely you cannot begin to believe such outrageous slander as that, sir, not after my years of loyal service."

That was enough to bring a faint smile to the Earl's lips. "And years of being privy to all the Duke's confidential matters as well. How curious that you, of all people, should be here when Lady Caroline arrives at an empty house. Pray, why don't you explain where her uncle and the servants have gone? Oh, and while you are at it, how did you come by those nasty scratches on your face?" He regarded his own roughened hands, then calmly held them out for inspection. "Afraid my nails are trimmed rather too short to inflict such damage. It is usually a lady's hand that leaves such marks."

The Duke frowned slightly.

"I am perfectly content to wait here until you are satisfied with the answers. Surely your secretary should be as well. If he is telling the truth."

Farrington took another step in the direction of the heavy oak door.

"A moment, Farrington."

"Your Grace, you cannot countenance the wild ravings of a desperate rogue," insisted his secretary. "We need to have him under lock and key as soon as possible. He's a very dangerous man, capable of anything—murder as well as treason. Why, he's left a trail of dead men in his wake. Let us not risk any more."

The Duke still hesitated.

Farrington paled imperceptibly.

Fatigue had caused Davenport to lean against the tall case clock, arms crossed over his chest. A grim expression appeared on his face at the irony of the other man's words.

"Trail of dead men," he repeated. "Well you should know about that. Lady Caroline and I have barely managed to avoid joining your other victims in journeying to the hereafter." As he shifted his weight, he started, then removed the packet from his shirt. He gave it a long, hard look before tossing it back on the side table. "You should be extremely proud of your daughter, sir. I cannot imagine another female—nay, anyone—with the courage and wits to endure what she has to bring this safely to your keeping." His gaze went to her still form.

Confusion clouded the Duke's face. The need for a reply

was forestalled, however, by the clatter of more footsteps on the entrance stairs and the entrance of his nephew, out of breath and nearly as disheveled as the Earl.

"Lucien!"

"I know you sent me on to Roxbury Manor, sir. But I met up with Darwin at the first posting inn. He told me Caro had left days ago and what she had in mind. When he received no word of her safe arrival, he set out to search for—" His eyes caught sight of the body on the floor. "Good Lord, who is the lad? What has happened here?"

"She has been struck—in the name of heaven, see that she is not seriously injured," replied the Duke.

Understanding dawned on Lucien's face. He rushed to kneel by his cousin's side and took her up in his arms. She stirred slightly.

"I think she is coming around."

An audible sigh of relief came from the Duke.

The Viscount looked up, aware for the first time of the others in the room. He nodded a brief acknowledgment at Farrington, then started on seeing the Earl.

"Why, hello, Julian. What the devil are you doing here?"

Davenport rubbed wearily at the scar on his cheek. "Bloody hell, I should have guessed," he muttered. "All those tales of a female cousin who could match any man at any exploit—we all thought you made up most of it, to keep us entertained. Well, you didn't tell the half."

Lucien managed a weak grin. "Ah, I take it that you have met Caroline when she was in possession of all her faculties, then?"

He couldn't catch exactly what the Earl said under his breath, but the Duke had no such problems in making himself understood.

"You are a friend of the Earl of Davenport?" he demanded of his nephew. "Lucien, I gave you more credit than to have any sort of association with a man of his character."

"But he's not Davenport—"

"I'm afraid I am."

"Oh. Charles stick his spoon in the wall?"

The Earl nodded. "Some months back."

There was a slight pause. "Can't say that I am sorry."

"Nor can I."

The Duke had followed the exchange with increasing puzzlement. "What utter nonsense are you talking about, Lucien? I recognize the fellow—"

"Twins," explained his nephew. "Julian isn't the one who is—or was—a rake. And he most certainly isn't the traitor we are searching for, that I'd stake my life on."

The discussion had diverted attention away from Farrington. Well aware that his chances for escape were dwindling with every passing moment, he intuitively recognized one last opportunity to turn disaster into triumph. With catlike agility, he lunged towards the Duke, catching him off guard. A hard shove sent the gentleman sprawling in the direction of his nephew. The pistols flew from his grip and clattered across the floor. Without missing a step, Farrington continued on, scooped up the object of all his efforts from the side table and raced for where the door stood half opened to the beckoning darkness of the night.

Suddenly the tall mahogany clock crashed to the floor, catching the fleeing man on the shoulder and knocking him off stride. It slowed him down just enough to allow the Earl to catch hold of his coat. With a strangled oath, Farrington was spun around just short of his only hope of escape.

As he did so, his arm slashed out in a wide arc. Davenport had forgotten about the knife and echoed the other man's obscenity as the blade cut a gash across his forearm. Still, he hung on and dragged Farrington to a standstill, though the force of the blow had knocked him to his knees. The knife came up again, light flashing off the razor-sharp edge.

Lucien, helpless with the weight of his cousin in his arms, cried out a warning.

"Oh, bloody hell," muttered Davenport, as he let go of the coat and threw himself to one side.

Farrington's desperate slash caught nothing but air. He tried to recover his balance, but the Earl was already on his feet and coming at him. A powerful right connected square on the secretary's jaw, dropping him to the floor like a sack of grain.

Davenport forgot his gentlemanly scruples long enough to add a kick to the ribs of the fallen man for good measure.

"That's for the lady," he murmured, as he bent to retrieve the packet from Farrington's senseless hand. On straightening up, he found the two beady eyes of the pistols trained on him, as well as the Duke's piercing gaze.

"Oh, put those damn things away," he growled. "I've had more than enough of guns and fists and cudgels and knives to last me for quite some time."

The Duke hesitated for only a fraction. A rueful smile crossed his lips as he let the weapons fall to his side.

Davenport limped over to him and put the documents into his hands. To his surprise, he noted that somehow half the packet had turned a dark crimson.

"Good Lord, Julian." Lucien was staring at his arm.

The Earl looked down at his blood-soaked sleeve and drew in his breath. "Would you mind telling your cousin that next time she takes it into her head to save the Empire, she may want to hire a regiment to keep up with her—it is beyond the power of one mere mortal."

Their startled expressions dissolved in a haze as he passed out cold.

* * *

The pain in his arm had subsided to a mere throbbing. As Davenport finished buttoning his shirt, he gingerly felt his ribs. They, too were less tender. Just a day's rest had him well on the mend, and a bath and shave had made him feel nearly human again. Clean clothes helped as well, he thought as he knotted the borrowed cravat. It was fortunate Lucien was nearly his height. At least he could appear in public without disgracing himself, a feat impossible to accomplish in his own tattered rags.

He stared in the mirror. So, everything had worked out in the end—the traitor was caught, the documents were safe and they had both come through it all more or less unscathed. Why, the maid delivering an early morning tray of tea had informed him that Lady Caroline was already up and about, despite the pleadings of the doctor and her family.

So why did he feel so glum?

A soft knock came at the door. It opened before he could voice a response, and a slim figure stole in with barely a rustle.

It took him a moment to recognize her. Gone were the breeches and loose shirt, replaced by an elegant gown of figured hunter-green silk. Even so, the willowy curves were unmistakable and the cut of the bodice, though hardly revealing, showed a good deal more of her flesh than he was used to seeing. The bruises had disappeared from her face, leaving her complexion unmarred for the first time since he had known her. The color had returned to her cheeks, only heightening the depth of her eyes, which were now fixing him with an all too familiar intensity.

He turned away to adjust his collar. "You must leave off visiting a man's chamber," he said in a gruff tone. "Surely you must know that sort of behavior can no longer be tolerated. The consequences would be . . ." His voice trailed off.

"Lucien told me you are leaving this morning."

"That's right."

"Were you not going to say good-bye?"

He shrugged.

The mirror reflected a glimpse of her brows drawing together. There was a pause, then she went on doggedly. "I never had a chance to . . . thank you."

He brushed out the wrinkles on his sleeve. "Consider it done. Now, you had better leave before anyone—"

Caroline put a hand on his arm. "Why are you acting as if we are complete strangers? I owe you my very life and—"

"I am being well paid for it," he said curtly. "That is, I assume you will honor your word. After all, it is evident you can well afford it."

The shock of his harsh words was immediately evident on her face. But she quickly schooled her features to reveal nothing further. "Your appearance and dress may have improved," she said coldly. "But your manners most certainly have not—you are still the most irritable, odious man I have ever had the misfortune of becoming acquainted with."

She dug into the pocket of her gown and withdrew a sheaf of banknotes. "Pray, count them to make sure you have not been shortchanged! I believe I have taken into account your horse. And I have added something extra for blood being drawn—that was not in our original agreement."

She flung the wad at his chest and stormed from the room. The exit was not quite as noiseless as the entrance, as the door came shut with a sound suspiciously akin to a slam.

Davenport winced, at both the sound and his own inexplicable behavior. He stared at the notes scattered over the expensive Aubusson carpet.

Damn the chit for having such an effect on him. Damn her for making him feel hot and cold, for sending his world spinning off kilter, for forcing him to confront emotions he wanted desperately to leave unvisited.

His boot kicked away the fortune at his feet, then he stalked from the room as well.

"Wonder why Julian bolted so quickly this morning," remarked Lucien as he helped himself to another slice of sirloin and refilled his cup from a steaming pot of tea the footman had just deposited near his elbow. "Looked like he could have used a decent meal, regardless of his hurry." He speared a kipper. "I know for certain that the Davenport town house is closed up tight. Any idea if he is staying in Town for long?"

Caroline didn't look up from slowly turning a piece of toast into crumbs. "I have no idea what Ju—Lord Davenport's plans are. I can't imagine why you should think he would inform me of his intentions, whatever they may be."

Her cousin's eyebrow shot up. "Well, the two of you did weather some rather tight spots."

She didn't answer, but raised her cup to her lips, studiously avoiding his gaze.

"When am I going to hear the full account? I've gotten only bits and pieces of the story from Uncle Thomas."

The cup came back to its saucer. "I'm sure you've heard the important parts. Farrington set two ruffians to ambush the coach. There was an accident. Poor John Coachman was killed. I was hurt somewhat but managed to make my escape. Lord Davenport found me, I recovered from my injuries at his estate, then he helped me get to London. It's as simple as that."

The eyebrow raised even higher. "Simple as that? You expect to foist such a Banbury tale off on me, cuz? Remember, I have a modicum of experience with your sort of adventures. 'Simple' is not quite the word I would ever choose."

Another piece of toast began to disintegrate onto her plate.

"It's odd," he continued. "Julian seemed to have no notion of who you were."

"I didn't tell him. Not exactly, that is."

"How did you convince him to take you to London in the face of such danger? Surely he demanded some sort of explanation?"

"He did. But then I offered him a goodly sum to serve as an escort. His pockets are well to let, you know, because of his brother."

Lucien's tone became incredulous. "You . . . hired the Earl of Davenport?"

"It was apparent he really needed the blunt," she muttered, then sought to deflect her cousin's line of questioning. "How is it you are acquainted with him?"

"Julian? Met him at Oxford. He got Tom Courtney and me out of a silly scrape, and we became friendly, though he's a bit senior to us. It's very like him, helping people out of a coil." His face became serious. "I wonder where Leighton has taken himself to? That's another of us that Julian took under his wing."

Finally her gaze came up to meet his. "Jeremy?" she exclaimed. "You know him as well?"

He nodded.

"What a prodigious talent!" Her eyes took on a speculative look. "Then you shall be pleased to help me with—"

"A simple story," he interrupted with a drawl. "Just how did it come about that you ran into Jeremy?" When he saw her mouth set into a mulish expression he merely shrugged. "Well, I imagine I shall hear it all at some time. It promises to be a good deal more intriguing than you are letting on at the moment. At least you were with someone capable of keeping you in one piece. Bang up to the mark, Julian is, don't you think?"

"Actually, I think the man is insufferable." She hoped her voice didn't sound quite as shrill as it did to her own ear.

Lucien regarded her thoughtfully. "Well, well."

"Well, what?"

"How interesting, is what I meant."

Two spots of color appeared on her cheeks. "What nonsense. I told you, I find Lord Davenport to be the most provoking of men."

"Ah, that is what is so interesting, my dear Caro." He tried unsuccessfully to repress a grin. "Normally you don't pay enough attention to the gentlemen around you to care one way or another about them."

Caroline stared in dismay at the ruins on her plate. She carefully wiped her fingers on the thick damask napkin, then rose with as much dignity as she could muster. "If you will excuse me, I have a number of pressing matters to attend to."

In the privacy of her own room, Caroline contemplated the pile of banknotes that the agitated young upstairs maid had promptly turned over to her keeping. Of course, she would see to it that they were delivered to Highwood. A bargain was a bargain. But the Earl's actions made no sense to her. Hadn't he made it coldly clear that he had endured her company for the sole purpose of earning the thousand pounds?

Yet he left it untouched, though the Lord knew he had dire need of it. She shook her head. Pride could cause one to act in the strangest ways, most of them having no connection at all to common sense, she mused, knowing full well that she was not unacquainted with the vagaries of such feelings. Still, it didn't seem the answer to all of the man's quirks.

Perhaps he didn't want to be beholden in any way to someone he held in . . . contempt. The possibility caused an unpleasant lurch in her stomach, though she chided herself that what the Earl thought of her should matter not a whit. It did, however. Somehow, the idea that he found her wanting in character or conduct was a blow more painful than any of the physical punishments she had received. Not that she could blame him on either account—she was honest enough to admit that.

Men simply didn't like a hopeless hoyden. Actually, she had figured that out long ago. And she was honest enough to admit she wasn't going to change, not for anyone. So that was that.

The only thing that remained a mystery to her was why he was so tender when she was in need and so harsh all the rest of the time. Hot and cold, like being warmed by the sun's rays one moment, only to be drenched by a chilling rain the next. Perhaps it had something to do with being an English gentleman.

Paper crackled as her fingers tightened around a handful of the banknotes. It was no use stewing over things she could not change. Putting aside all thoughts of the Earl of Davenport, Caroline vowed to turn her attention to a matter she could act on.

Chapter Eleven

They are truly marvelous," said Caroline softly. "It will be a stunning success, of that I have no doubt."

The gentleman on whose arm her hand rested made a coughing sound. When he turned his head, his eyes were clouded with doubt. "Do you really think so?" He let out his breath with something like a sigh. "I hardly know what to expect. If you must know the truth, my knees are quaking so badly it is a wonder I can stand upright. What if everyone hates them?"

She smiled and gave him a reassuring pat. "Most unlikely." Then her expression became more serious, taking on a degree of pensiveness. "Are artists always so afraid of what the critics might say?"

They came to a halt after viewing the last of the paintings and Jeremy Leighton mulled over the question at length. "It is difficult to explain," he finally answered. "I mean, if you believe in yourself, that is all that really matters. But one can't help feeling terribly—pardon the expression—naked, with one's soul hanging up for all to see."

"That is a frightening thought," she agreed. "I hadn't ever thought of it quite like that. But still, I think you have very little to worry about. What you show of yourself is a strength, compassion and lyricism that would do anyone credit."

Jeremy colored nearly as brightly as one of the deftly rendered sunsets hung on the wall behind him. He dropped his head to mask his embarrassment at the compliment as well as his lingering apprehension as to the reception of his work.

"I cannot thank you enough, Lady Caroline, for arranging all of this." He gestured at the impressive exhibition space. "Without your influence and . . ."

She cut off what promised to be a lengthy—and effusive—speech. "My influence would have meant nothing had you not had the talent to impress the Academy. Not for all the peers of the realm would they hang a show they did not feel was worthy of such a display. You shall see for yourself at the opening later today, and at the ball we are giving in your honor tonight. No doubt you shall be the toast of the town."

His face became even more scarlet as he dug for something in his pocket.

"I have a . . . token of my thanks," he mumbled, pressing a small package, wrapped carefully in patterned paper, into her hands.

"May I open it now?"

He nodded.

Caroline tore away the gold and indigo covering to reveal an oval miniature framed in polished ebony.

"It is a . . . very good likeness," she faltered as she stared down at the familiar features. Her voice sounded strained, tentative, even to her own ears. There was a long silence as she searched for something appropriate to say. Then at last her eyes rose to meet his.

"He looks very unhappy."

"He is." Jeremy cleared his throat. "He invited me to stay with him for a while after he had returned from London so I am well aware of his current state of mind."

"Have things not been going well at Highwood?" she asked quickly. "I had thought that with the additional funds, his most pressing problems would at least be lessened."

"I do not think it is solely estate matters which are preying on his mind."

Caroline turned slightly, as if suddenly taking a great interest in the expansive landscape hanging to her left. There was another long silence. The conversation was heading into dangerous waters as far as she was concerned. But tempting as it was to steer clear of discussing anything to do with the Earl, she decided such a course would be cowardly.

"I am sorry if I have upset his lordship, with all the trouble he has endured on my account. Are his wounds—"

"His injuries have nothing to do with it, either," interrupted Jeremy.

To her dismay, she, too, experienced a rush of hot color washing over her cheeks. "I can't, that is, I . . ." Why was she reduced to stammering like a miss scarcely out of the schoolroom? she wondered. Giving herself a mental shake, she composed her emotions enough to continue in a more coherent manner. "I can't imagine that I should have any effect on the Earl's mood now—why, he was only too glad to rid himself of my presence, I assure you. In fact, he rushed off from Town as soon as he was physically able. I can't say that I blame him. After all, he was either cutting up something fierce at me or having to risk his neck to pull my irons out of the fire. I guess all I ever seemed to do was turn his world upside down."

There was a glimmer of a smile from Jeremy. "Indeed. That you certainly did."

At a loss for words, Caroline bit her lip and stole another look at the painting in her hands.

The gesture was enough to encourage Jeremy to screw up his courage and speak more forthrightly than he normally would have dared.

"You know, it seems to me that Julian is so used to taking care of other people's welfare that he has little experience in seeing to his own. Mayhap what has him at sixes and sevens these days is the realization that he is not as immune to the need for someone to truly care for him as he has wished to think. And mayhap he doesn't quite know how to deal with it."

Caroline made a strangled sound at the back of her throat.

"Forgive me if I overstep myself." His voice dropped to nearly a whisper. "It's just that I wish to see two people I care about . . ."

She was saved from having to make a reply by the sudden appearance of her cousin.

His boots rapped out a staccato measure of impatience as he crossed the polished marble floor. "Have you two lost all track of time?" he called. "I have been walking my grays outside for more than a quarter hour!" he made a show of consulting his pocket watch. "We shall barely have time to return home and dress for the opening."

"Perhaps I shall leave the two of you to attend—you can tell me all about it later," said Jeremy faintly.

"Hah!" Lucien took him firmly by the arm and began marching him towards the door. Caroline followed close behind, grateful for the chance to elude the sharp gaze of her cousin for a moment and to mask the utter confusion caused by Jeremy's words.

"Buck up your courage, man," continued Lucien. "It can't be as bad as you think."

Jeremy cast him a baleful look.

"You will have your good friends to lend moral support."

"I wonder if Julian shall be able to attend . . ."

"Count on it, he will be here," assured the young Viscount. "I sent my own carriage to fetch him, along with two of our largest footmen who had orders to see he arrived today, even if they had to truss him like a sow for market to accomplish the feat. He will be staying with us too, of course. Uncle wouldn't hear of anything else."

Caroline's stomach gave a little lurch. She hurriedly stuffed the miniature into her reticule as Lucien turned to hand her into the waiting town coach. Jeremy had every reason to feel weak in the knees.

What was her excuse?

Davenport stared out at the increasing number of vehicles clogging the road. The carriage had finally been forced to slacken its breakneck pace on reaching the outskirts of London. Still, they would arrive at their destination in more than enough time. He shifted against the soft leather squabs, his scowl only deepening on taking in the sights and sounds that signalled the change from country to city. He was in a sour mood and the innumerable hours he had been forced to spend alone with his thoughts throughout the journey had merely served to exacerbate it.

It had been damned unfair of Lucien to force him into this, he fumed as he crossed one booted leg over the other, though a slight prick of conscience made him admit that he wouldn't, in any case, have missed Jeremy's opening for the world. The sight of the worn and cracked leather caused his mouth to set in a tight line. As if he needed any reminder of his financial straits. At least he had a halfway decent set of evening clothes so that he wouldn't be totally humiliated at the reception—or the Duke's ball.

It was the contemplation of the coming evening, not the opening of Jeremy's exhibition, that had the Earl in such a black humor. Given his druthers, it was an event he would have avoided like the plague, but the Viscount had given him little choice in the matter. Short of punching the deadlights out of the two burly footmen—a task he was by no means sure he could accomplish in his present condition—he was now in thrall to the Duke's hospitality. And that meant dutifully taking part in the gala festivities, regardless of his personal feelings on the matter.

His fingers drummed on the frayed material of his breeches.

Very well. He might be forced to make an appearance.

But nobody could force him to like it.

And nobody could force him to pay the least attention to a certain other person sure to be in attendance. A vision of a willowy form, gowned in the height of fashion, hair dressed becomingly in a soft, feminine style danced unbidden into his head. With an audible growl he tried to banish it from his thoughts. However, he had learned over the course of more than a few long, empty nights that mere words had little effect—it took at least a bottle or two of brandy to chase away the memory of the exact tilt of her head, the curve of her breasts, the radiance of her smile.

An oath escaped his lips. Then suddenly they curved upward into an ironic smile. Why, the chit had him literally talking to himself. Next thing they would be hauling him off to Bedlam, which would no doubt be an appropriate fate if things continued on as they had been going. At Highwood he had been able to use physical exhaustion stirred with a liberal dose of spirits to keep his mind occupied. But as the carriage rolled closer to its final destination, he decided he could no longer avoid facing his real feelings.

He had fought hard against admitting it, but it now seemed futile to deny his heart was lost. And the fact of the matter was he was afraid. So terribly afraid that his mouth went dry at the very thought of how much she meant to him, and his limbs felt as weak as jellied eel. He had been rejected once by someone he cared for—and in favor of someone like his brother. No matter that Helen had come to bitterly regret her choice. She had made it of her own free will at the time. He wasn't sure he could endure such pain again. So it seemed better to make sure another lady would never have to make that choice.

Oh yes, he had made quite sure of that.

There was no longer any reason to go on deluding himself, pretending throughout the long, lonely evenings with only the bottle for company that he preferred it that way. No reason to pretend that she was not at all the type of lady he desired—too outspoken, too hoydenish, too opinionated, too headstrong. At least he could now be honest with himself about that. He missed her more than he could ever have imagined. Life seemed sadly flat without the dimension she brought to his existence. But there was little use in pining over what could never be. All he could hope for was that his behavior of late had ensured that Lady Caroline Alexandra Georgina Talcott, heiress and daughter of one of the most powerful men in the country, would not even acknowledge the presence of the ill-tempered, penniless Earl whose sullied reputation only highlighted how unsuitable a connection between them was.

Even now, he had to wince at the memory of his cold words, her wounded expression. Surely she would stay well away from him. And surely he could keep up the charade of not caring for one more evening.

But it was going to be a very long evening.

The grand room was awash in the flickering light of countless candles. The soft fragrance of tuber roses wafted through the trill of laughter, the buzz of conversation and the lilting notes of a violin as the musicians began the first notes of the opening dance. It was quite a crush, as one turbaned matron had remarked to another, once settled with their glasses of ratafia punch. Nobody wanted to miss the opportunity to meet the gifted young artist whose praises were being trumpeted throughout town. It did not do his reputation any harm that a vague hint of intrigue concerning certain affairs of state had attached themselves to his name. Half the young ladies of the *ton* had abandoned their allegiance to a certain poet and proclaimed their fascination with the even more romantic young painter.

Caroline had to repress a smile at the sight of yet another gentleman seeking to introduce his giddy sister to Jeremy Leighton. After the requisite small talk, her friend managed to extricate himself from the crowd and take a brief respite in leading her out for a waltz.

"As you see, you had little cause for worry," she said close by his ear as the melody began in earnest.

Jeremy's expression appeared glazed, but at least his feet managed the steps without a major mishap. "I can't fathom . . ." he began.

Caroline laughed out loud. "Don't try. Why not just enjoy the moment? We all know how quickly things can change."

He thought he detected a note of wistfulness in her voice but refrained from remarking on it. Instead he looked around at the whirl of elegant ladies and gentlemen and shook his head slightly. "I don't know. I hardly feel comfortable here. I wish I were back in my studio . . ."

"You soon will be, though I imagine you will be able to work in a good deal more comfort than before. No doubt you will be having to turn away commissions from now on."

His eyes still roamed the room. "You know, my parents are here. They have become reconciled to the notion that their son is a painter and not an officer of the Royal Navy. I have you to thank for making this dream of mine come true." His one good hand tightened on hers. "I wish I could help make a dream come true for you."

Her lips trembled imperceptibly. "Why, Jeremy, how kind of you, but I have no need for dreams."

His brows drew together slightly as he wondered how truthful her words were.

"I believe you are engaged for the next set with Miss Henley," said Caroline as the music came to an end and they drifted from the dance floor. A petite blonde dressed in an expensive gown of figured white silk embroidered with cornflowers was staring with a rapt, mooncalf expression at the young artist.

Jeremy blanched. "Oh, God," he muttered under his breath and darted a pleading look at his companion.

Caroline checked the urge to laugh out loud as she left him to his fate. Ducking a bevy of her own admirers, she pleaded the need to absent herself in order to confer with her father's major domo to make sure everything was running as it ought. Yet as she neared the door to the card room, she paused for a moment, half hidden by an arrangement of potted palms. Her eyes scanned the vast ballroom, searching carefully among the shimmering silks, glittering jewels and impeccably tailored evening coats. She hadn't realized she was holding her breath until it came out in a sigh of disappointment.

He wasn't there.

She had caught a glimpse of him earlier at the opening of Jeremy's exhibition, but their paths hadn't crossed, not close enough for conversation. It was almost as if he was avoiding having to exchange even the simplest of greetings.

To her chagrin, she felt the sting of tears. Jeremy might possess an artist's rare gift of being able to quickly discern the true emotions of a person, but in the case of a certain individual, his observations were way off the mark. The Earl might be unhappy, but it had little to do with her—or at least, not in the way Jeremy imagined. Clearly Lord Davenport had no wish to further their . . .

Their what?

Did she dare call it friendship? Whatever it was, it was something so special to her that she missed it with an ache infinitely worse than all the physical punishment she had endured.

But this was neither the time nor place to think such thoughts. Mustering all of her considerable will, she pasted a smile back on her face and turned towards the corridor. A short stroll to check on the quantity of champagne was an excellent idea. Perhaps she would even help herself to a glass afterwards, in hopes of adding some effervescence to her flat spirits.

It was only from the corner of her eye that she caught his intense gaze. He, too, was alone, his dark coat and pantaloons allowing him to blend into the shadows cast by the potted trees. He had been observing her, that much was evident. For just an instant, she beheld the look in his eyes, before his face once again took on a familiar scowl and he turned his head, without so much as a nod.

Her heart caught in her throat. Was it possible?

A hand reached out for hers. She scarcely heard Lord Appleby remind her that the pleasure of the next country set was his. The steps seemed to go on interminably and it seemed like an age before the final note was struck. Thankfully, a waltz was next. A waltz promised to Lucien. As her cousin approached, she took his arm and proceeded away from the dance floor rather than towards it.

"You must release me from this dance," she said in a low voice. "I must tend to a pressing matter with one of our guests."

Lucien raised an eyebrow but refrained from raking her over the coals concerning her rather odd request. He merely shrugged and announced his intention of using the time to filch a bottle of champagne from the cellars so that he and Lord Knightly might fill their glasses a tad more often— and fully—than the waiters had been instructed to do.

Caroline looked past the palms. He was still there, still alone, still looking as black as a windswept sea. It was the scowl that made her take heart. Before her courage could desert her, she hurried towards him. Seeing as his back was against the wall he had no chance to escape.

"Good evening, my lord."

Davenport gave a slight start of surprise, then muttered a passably civil greeting in turn.

"I thought, for old time's sake, I might take up the role of a man again long enough to ask you for the next dance."

His face betrayed a warring of emotions.

She swallowed hard. Perhaps she had been mistaken after all. "Of course, if you would rather not . . ."

By way of answer he took firm hold of her elbow and ushered her out onto the polished parquet. Suddenly he was quite close. She could feel the warmth emanating from his broad chest, the pressure of his hand on the small of her back. As the captivating strains of the music filled the room, the Earl began to move with the lilting tempo, guiding their steps with lithe grace.

Caroline followed his lead effortlessly. For a moment, she closed her eyes, giving herself over entirely to the pressure of his hands, the measured strength of his long legs. Attuned as she was to the nuances of his touch, she felt the tension begin to ebb out of his limbs as they glided across the floor. When at last she ventured to look up at him, she saw the color of his eyes had cleared, though the strange intensity still lingered.

Though loath to break the harmony between them at that moment, she felt compelled to break the silence. Suddenly unsure of how to begin, she blurted out the first thing that came to mind.

"Speaking of gentlemen, I asked Lucien about the song . . ."

Davenport's brow furrowed in puzzlement.

"Remember? You wouldn't tell me what a sodomite was. You told me to ask my cousin. Well, I did."

The Earl nearly tripped over his own feet.

"But he wouldn't explain either," she continued, ignoring the incredulous look on his face. "He said he had a good mind to call you out for exposing me to such language. I still don't—"

The laugh began softly at the back of his throat, then reached such a volume as to draw inquiring glances from the couples around them.

"You are still utterly incorrigible," he said with a shake of his head.

Caroline drew in her breath. She had approached the Earl with the intention of being charming and ladylike, but somehow things had gone awry—as usual. Her cheeks reddened, but she decided as she had already made a mull of things, there was no harm in going on.

"I know you find me totally lacking in delicate sensibilities, sir, and that you tolerated our acquaintance because you needed the money, but . . ."

He opened his mouth as if to speak.

". . . but I still want to thank you for all you have done for me." She smiled a little crookedly. "And to tell you that I shall greatly miss your company—despite everything, we had some fun."

"You have a rather odd notion of fun," he murmured, his voice still rich with humor. His hand tightened on hers, and the odd look came back to his eyes. "I . . ."

His sense of timing, flawless up to that moment, suddenly deserted him, for just then, the music came to an end.

There was a milling about as couples around them began to glide from the dance floor. A voice boomed out from crowd. "Julian! Haven't seen you in an age. Meant to congratulate you on the title, don't you know." A gentleman of imposing girth, sporting a canary-yellow waistcoat which only emphasized the size of his stomach, appeared to give substance to the words. "Though of course, perhaps 'congratulate' isn't the right word, given the circumstances—brother and all. Still, you'll be a far better Earl than Charles, if I may say so."

He and his partner fell in step beside Caroline and the Earl, oblivious to the spasm of frustration that crossed Davenport's face.

"Kind of you, Stanfield," muttered the Earl as he sought to steer away from the man and his partner.

"Come, let us have a glass of champagne together after we have delivered these lovely young ladies to the lucky men next in line for their company," continued the man as he gave a jovial wink to the amply endowed matron by his side.

The Earl clenched his teeth to keep from snapping an uncivil reply. He turned to Caroline. "As I was saying . . ." he began in a low voice.

Stanfield finished making an elaborate bow to his lady. Straightening with some difficulty, he clamped a beefy hand around the Earl's elbow and led him away.

Well, thought Caroline, that was that.

She managed to make a perfect cake of herself. Drat Jeremy for encouraging her to think the Earl might harbor any feelings other than disapproval of both her character and her conduct. Her words—all of them—had merely shocked him, though by now he should have gotten used to her unbridled tongue. The only saving grace was that in all likelihood, it hadn't been possible to sink any lower in his regard than before she opened her mouth. Still, she wondered what he was about to say before the unfortunate interruption. There had been something about his expression. . . . She sighed. No doubt he was merely going to give her another set-down, spelling out in great detail her copious faults.

She was saved from having to dwell any further on such lowering thoughts as a smiling young gentleman stepped up to take her hand for the next dance.

Davenport watched her being led out for yet another set and took a long swallow of champagne. It seemed her dance card was, if anything, oversubscribed. His eyes narrowed at the sight of the cluster of eligible young lords hanging on her every move, more than willing to take up any slack in attentiveness. The chances of having a private word with her dwindled with every passing note of the violin.

He forced himself to watch her movements—steps full of life, head tilted so that curling tendrils brushed the nape of her neck, hips swaying in a way that sent a rush of heat through him. Draining the rest of his glass did nothing to quench it. Of course she would be surrounded by a bevy of admirers. She was an heiress—and a damnably attractive one, though most of the young louts probably didn't understand that her appeal transcended mere prettiness. It was her indomitable spirit that had him near baying at the moon. . . .

"Hello, Julian. Quite the evening. Enjoying yourself?"

Davenport started at Lucien's words, then merely glowered at him.

"Glad you could make it," continued the young Viscount cheerfully as he refilled both the Earl's glass and his own.

"Hmmph." Davenport clamped his lips together, determined to avoid any conversation. He was not in the mood, nor was he in charity with the young man at the moment. But for Lucien, he would be safely ensconced in front of his own hearth, with only his own visions of her to torment himself, not the real thing.

Seemingly oblivious to the Earl's cool reception, Lucien drained his glass in one swallow and turned his eyes to his cousin.

"Jackanapes, all of them," he announced as he watched a thin Marquess with his hair cut *à la* Brutus lead Caroline through the steps of a country dance.

Davenport couldn't hide a look of surprise.

Lucien smiled. "No bottom to any of 'em. They're all scared to death of her. Wouldn't do at all."

"What wouldn't?" asked the Earl, in spite of his resolve to remain indifferent to the Viscount's chatter.

"No, wouldn't do at all." Lucien went on as if he hadn't heard. "What she needs is someone who'll have the sense to let her ride neck and leather with him. Oh, maybe he'll have to rein her in a bit now and then, but who of us doesn't need a little guidance at times? Point is, she's a rare spirit. Well, I know it won't be easy, but nothing worth having ever is."

Davenport shifted his weight uncomfortably. "I believe you're foxed."

Lucien studied his empty glass. "I have probably drunk more than my uncle would have wished, but less than I intend to before the night is done. It is a celebration, after all."

"Yes, Jeremy deserves it."

"Indeed he does. Jeremy took a chance. Bravo for him! He had the guts to pursue what he wanted, regardless of how daunting the odds might have seemed." The bubbles frothed up once again in the Viscount's glass. "Here's to taking chances, eh? Better to do that than be a coward and wonder for all one's life about what might have been." He threw back the contents and, with an enigmatic smile, left the Earl in a state of even greater discomfiture than before.

Another glance showed Caroline twirling around in the arms of some other gentleman, her graceful neck arched in laughter at some murmured pleasantry. Deciding that the evening was going from bad to worse, Davenport banged his own glass down and retired to sulk in the privacy of his own bedchamber.

Midnight had long since passed before Caroline was able to cry off from dancing. The number of guests was finally beginning to dwindle and the musicians were showing signs of putting down their instruments for the last time. The evening had been a great success. Jeremy would no doubt find himself with more commissions than he could ever accept. So at least she had managed to be a positive influence in someone's life, she mused, as her eyes involuntarily darted to a certain corner of the ballroom.

Just as quickly she chided herself for being such a goose. How silly to have thought he might have remained to finish their conversation.

"Come, maybe this will lighten your spirits, cuz." Lucien placed a glass of champagne into her hands, then slipped his arm in hers and led her to a more private spot. She was about to open her mouth in protest when he cut her off.

"A stunning success, Caro, m'dear. Jeremy appears as sought after as a diamond of the first water with twenty thousand a year. A toast is in order." By now his speech had become a trifle slurred, but his feet were steady under him as he raised his own glass to his lips.

Caroline peered at his flushed face. "Oh dear, Luce, I fear you are well in your cups. Pray, try to avoid Papa, so he doesn't ring a peal over your head."

He grinned. "I think he'll forgive me this one transgression. After all, this is a special evening, with much to celebrate—Jeremy. The documents staying out of that snake Farrington's hands. Your safe return. Oh, and your future happiness."

Her head shot up. "What . . ."

"Saw Julian earlier. Told him he was a damn fool if he didn't offer for you."

"You didn't!" she gasped.

"I did," he asserted. "Well, not in so many words, but he is no slowtop. I am sure he took my meaning."

Caroline colored with mortification. "I could strangle you, Lucien, truly I could," she said in a tight voice.

"Oh, fustian. A fine big brother I'd be if I didn't look out for your happiness—you *are* in love with him, aren't you?"

She made a strangled sound.

"Thought so." He grinned again, and the mischief there melded with affection. "I like Julian. What's more, I respect him. Always have. Just the fellow for you, since you won't have me."

Caroline's color was now akin to that of a boiled beet. "You really are addled in your cockloft," she sputtered. "Why, he doesn't even like me above half . . ."

"Has he kissed you?"

She stopped in mid-sentence, her expression changing from one of indignation to one of being caught out. "It didn't mean anything," she finally managed to mutter.

Lucien laughed out loud—overlong to Caroline's ear. She was spared further embarrassment by the approach of her father.

"I think I shall take a stroll in the garden. I could do with a breath of fresh air," he whispered, giving her a broad wink.

"Coward!" she hissed.

"It's called strategy, m'dear. I'm getting rather good at it, don't you think?" With those parting words, he disappeared in the shadows.

The Duke slipped his arm where Lucien's had just rested. "Now where has that young scamp taken himself off to?"

"He's gone to clear his head." There was a touch of asperity in her voice.

Her father gave a chuckle. "I can well imagine why he wishes to avoid me." Then his head cocked to one side. "Now what has he done to overset you?"

She gave a deep sigh. "Oh, it is of no matter. Just his usual teasing."

He opened his mouth as if to say something, then seemed to change his mind. Instead, he surveyed the nearly empty room. The flickering candles were burning low, but their soft glow still shed light over the festive array of flowers, the glasses of champagne still bubbling with good cheer.

"You have done well, my dear. I am proud of you for showing such a kindness to your friend."

Caroline looked up at him in surprise.

"I am proud of you in so many other ways as well," continued the Duke in a halting voice. "Perhaps I don't . . . well, that is . . ."

Her surprise only deepened as she watched her father struggle for words in a way that was most unlike him.

"Lucien brought up the fact that you may have the oddest notion that . . . that perhaps I might, well, regret that you are not a . . ." He took a deep breath. "I can't imagine a more nonsensical thing. Surely you must know that." He gave her a hard squeeze. "Perhaps I don't give voice to my feelings as easily as some other men, but no father could be blessed with a more wonderful child—intrepid, intelligent, full of integrity. My dear Caro, you are the light of my life." At that his arms came around her in a fierce hug.

She blinked back tears as her cheek rested against his shoulder. "Oh Papa."

For a time, neither of them said anything as they just held each other.

Then she raised her head. "It seems Lucien has decided he should take over the ordering of my life," she said rather shakily.

Her father smiled. "Mayhap he has more sense than I give him credit for."

Caroline wiped at her cheeks. "Men," she sniffed. "They always think they know best."

The Duke dropped a kiss on her brow. "Ah, but we are quite quickly—and frequently—corrected of that delusion."

Davenport rubbed at his temples. His head felt as if a score of revelers had danced the night away on it despite the fact that he had not imbibed overly much throughout the past evening. Or was it still the same evening? It seemed he had lost track of all time as he lay tossing and turning in his bed, unable to fall into even a fitful slumber. He finally gave up even trying. Throwing off the covers, he rose and went to stand by the window, staring out into the blackness that still enveloped the terraced garden.

The images of dancers refused to bow out of his head. Caroline with this man. Caroline with that man. He wasn't sure what was worse—imagining her in the arms of someone else or having to endure the actual sight of her there. Things seemed to him to be as black as the outside, until one small ray of light pierced through his dark musings.

She had told him she would miss him. Despite his ill-temper, his horrible moods and rough words, she still could say that. Maybe there was hope yet.

Hope of what? His fingers drummed on the window casing. Perhaps it was high time to be entirely honest with himself. Much as he had tried to convince himself otherwise over the past few months, the thought of life without her was much like tumbling into an unfathomable abyss. And wasn't the notion of such an empty existence even more frightening than the possibility of rejection? If he didn't try, he would despise himself as a coward for the rest of his days. For cowardly was how he had been acting, and she deserved better than that. She had never backed away from her fears or doubts. She had the courage to say what she felt. He should do no less, no matter if she laughed in his face or told him to go to the devil.

His mouth quirked ruefully on trying to imagine just

what her reaction to his declaration would be. Somehow she seemed to be under the cork-brained impression that he didn't have . . . any regard for her. Well, he had his work cut out for him. But for some odd reason he couldn't lay a finger on, he suddenly felt more at peace with himself than he had for ages.

He returned to his bed and fell into a deep sleep as soon as he closed his eyes.

A soft knock on the door interrupted Davenport's second attempt to arrange the folds of his neckcloth just so. He didn't usually fuss over matters of dress but this morning he wanted to be at his best. Sighing, he left off struggling with the length of linen and bade the maid to come in. Indeed, he was looking forward to the early morning cup of coffee that he had requested be brought to his chamber each day— being a guest in such a well-run household as that of the Duke had its little privileges.

He turned from the mirror, ready to voice his thanks, only to have his mouth drop in surprise at the sight of Caroline standing before him instead of the expected servant.

"Before you begin bear-jawing at me," she said in a rush, "I know I am behaving like a hoyden again, coming to your room and all, but I simply *had* to speak with you, before you left for Highwood." She hesitated while she took in a gulp of air. "Lucien told me last night that he had given you the idea—that is, he suggested to you that you should . . ." The color rose to her face and her eyes dropped away from his. "Drat it," she stammered. "What I mean to say is, he told me he had tried to cajole you into . . . making an offer to me. I can't imagine where he got the notion that . . ."

"Would it be so very terrible if I did?" asked the Earl, barely louder than a whisper.

Her eyes came up slowly. "But you don't even *like* me! I mean, you can't forget that I stole your horse, called you all sorts of rude names, drank out of the bottle like a fishmonger, not to speak of making you drag me out of the mud, or putting your life at risk time and again."

"No," he agreed. "I can't forget those things. Neither can I forget the way you brandished a pistol at four men to save my skin or how you tended my wound . . . or how you called out my name as I held you in my arms. I don't *ever* want you to call out another man's name like that."

The expression in his eyes made the breath catch in her throat.

His own breathing had become a bit ragged as well. "Don't like you?" he continued. "Why, I think I've been in love with you ever since you planted your fist on my nose that first morning I met you."

"You have?" she said a bit uncertainly. "You mean you don't think I—"

"I mean that I want you to marry me, my dear Caroline."

"Are you sure? Because I doubt I shall be able to change much—I shall always be headstrong and outspoken." Her mouth quivered just the tiniest fraction. "Perhaps you should tire of having to pick me up out of the mud."

Suddenly she was in his arms. "I shall never tire of it, my love," he said as he planted kisses on the lobe of her ear. "Indeed, life would be sadly flat without having to try and keep up with you." Then he turned serious. "You think you can put up with all my faults? For I, too, fear I shall remain a growling bear at times. And you are all too aware of the state of my finances. I can hardly offer you the life to which you are accustomed."

Caroline ran her hand along the thin white line of his scar. "Julian," she said simply. "Oh, Julian."

Then she lifted her lips to his.

When finally they parted, his eyes were a mezmerising shade of blue she had never seen before.

"Is that a yes?" he ventured.

She smiled in answer. "If you hadn't spoken today, I might have been forced to follow you to Highwood and put on breeches again so that I could ask you myself."

"You may wear breeches anytime you wish. You may ride neck and leather, you may drain bottles upon bottles of brandy, you may curse like a sailor—just as long as you do all those things with me."

Caroline blinked back tears of joy. "Why, I can't imagine a life without you. I do love you so—" The rest of her words were cut off by another kiss.

A soft knock came at the door. Without waiting for an answer, Lucien entered. "Julian . . ." he began, then stopped short at the sight of his cousin wrapped most intimately in the Earl's embrace. A sly grin spread over his lips as he crossed his arms over his chest. "Well, I assume the two of you know what this means."

Davenport made no attempt to release her. "I know very well what it means, and so do you."

"Was this your final strategy, cuz?" demanded Caroline. "Just in case the subtle suggestions didn't work? How dare you follow me—"

Lucien's mouth twitched. "I have no idea what you are talking about. I came in here to speak to Julian on a very important matter."

"And what was that?"

"Why, to be the first to wish him happy, of course." The grin widened. "Either that, or to call him out, though I'm not sure which a sane man would consider the lesser of two evils—facing my much improved aim or being leg-shackled to you for a lifetime."

Caroline gave an indignant yelp and looked for something to throw at her cousin.

Lucien winked at the Earl. "I take it I may wish you happy?"

Davenport chuckled as his arms tightened around Caroline's waist. "You may, indeed." His lips then brushed close to her ear and the rest of his words were murmured for only her to hear.

"For no one in the world could be happier, my love."